YANG- A WINGS OF DIABLO MC NOVEL- NEW ORLEANS CHAPTER

RAE B. LAKE

ACKNOWLEDGMENTS

To My Best Choice - I can't say that we were the most obvious choice or even the easiest but I will say that you were the best choice for me. I see you, through all the nonsense and anger, I see who you truly are and I'm grateful you are here taking this ride with me.

To my little Ice Queens- I'm so happy that you all are growing up to know exactly what you want and how to get it. I've never been one to fight for what should rightfully be mine, that is until I had you two. Keep on fighting and keep on making momma proud!

To my Friends, Family and Readers- I really had so much fun writing this story. The words seemed to flow right out of me and I felt such a strong connection with Ice. I hope you love it as much as I do.

DISCLAIMER

This book includes several graphic traumatic events that may be troubling/triggering for some readers. Discretion is advised.

CHAPTER

YANG

"Come on, you fucking cheat! The balls are weighted!"

"Sir, I promise you that the ball is standard weight and size. Better luck next time."

"That's bullshit! I watched it jump from one slot to the next after it was settled. You're a cheat!" The man steps into the dealers face and that was my cue to get him the fuck out. When I walk into the casino no one expects me to be one of the members who owns it. From my kutte to my low-key demeanor nothing about me screams casino owner. This motherfucker is about to find out exactly why no one is allowed to act up in my casino.

I grab the man by the back of his neck and squeeze hard enough for him to cringe. His skin is oily and I can feel his pulse beating a million miles a minute. "You got a fucking problem with how my dealer is doing his job?"

The troublemaker turns as best he can in my direction and looks into my calm eyes.

"No, I don't have a problem. I was just giving my observation. I'm sorry. I should have just left with what I had left." He stutters and drops the tone of his voice to a more respectful one.

I release the man and turn him so he is facing me. "That's what I thought. Of course, the Wings want you to have the best experience here in the casino, so I'll take your observation into account." I wipe my hands down the man's shirt fixing any wrinkles I created while making sure he knows that I will fuck him up if he gets out of line. "For tonight, I believe you've had just about enough excitement. Maybe you should be on your way?" I glare at him and wait for him to make the right decision. The decision to move the fuck out of my line of sight before shit gets really ugly.

"Yes, sir. I'm leaving now, thank you. Sorry about that." He stutters and picks up his coat from the back of the chair he was sitting on. He drops it two more times before he turns and starts to speed walk away from me. He looks over his shoulder just as many times to make sure I'm still there watching him. I didn't have the time to keep tabs on him. We had security for shit like that.

I look to the northeast corner and get the lead guard's attention. He comes over to me quickly as he should. As the Sergeant at Arms of the Wings of Diablo MC and a co-owner of the Gold Wings Casino, it's my job to make sure shit is being run correctly. My club sets the rules and I expect every single one of them to be followed.

"Follow that man out. He's not allowed back in tonight."

"Yes, sir." With that the security guard walks off, using his walkie talkie to alert and coordinate with the other members of the security team.

"How long was he here causing problems?" I ask the man running the roulette station.

"Just a few rounds. It escalated quickly."

"Did you not think to address the problem? If he was accusing you of cheating, you either get someone to switch out with you or you call over the pit boss. Don't stand there and let the other patrons believe that the game is rigged. Either you're stupid or you just don't know how to do your job, next time something like this happens, you're out of here. You get it?"

The dealer swallows down hard before he answers, "Yes, sir. I understand."

I call over the pit boss and have the dealer changed out as well as the ball in case there are any players who might have witnessed the little interaction. Casinos are all about the player having a good time. It's our job to make sure that happens.

It's well past three in the morning but ever since that shit went down with Mark, someone always accompanies Pirate on his pick ups. This week it was my turn. I stare at the door that leads into the main vault area; this shit was taking way too long. I'm tired and want to get back to the clubhouse for some much needed rest.

Everyone has been on edge since our run in with René, me included. It's rare that anything bothers me enough to stress me the fuck out like this has. Though I guess when you might have a dead man running around with a vendetta it can work on your nerves.

"What the fuck, the bastard forget how to fucking count or

what?" I mumble more to myself than anyone else. I'm supposed to stay out on the floor and make sure that no one is scouting the place or looks to be out of place. With it being this late at night it's easy to see anyone who might be up to some shady shit. I look over my shoulder a second before I enter in the 13 digit passcode and the door opens. I'm met by two fully armed guards who do their sweep of me and then let me proceed.

"I'm coming … I'm coming." Pirate says out loud before I can even get one word out of my mouth.

"What the hell is taking so long? We should be in and out of here within fifteen minutes tops. Staying this long in one place is just asking to get jacked."

Pirate's eyes pop up to mine, "Yang, you remember who I am right? I know everything there is to know about cash, more importantly our club's cash. If I need a few extra minutes, then I think I should be able to take it. Unless there is something I don't know?"

I glare at him for a second before I roll my eyes and turn to face the large two-way mirror. "There is nothing that you don't know Pirate. Just hurry the hell up." It's my fault shit was getting old. A few months back when we were still deep in our fight with René and his fucked up cronies, Pirate had sent one of our prospects to do a pick up for him. That pick up was the last thing Mark would ever be ordered to do. He was burned alive along with several casino workers and their families. Since then, Pirate has taken his job as Treasurer above and beyond. Always feeling that we thought what had happened was his fault.

We knew it wasn't, the old bastard just needed to get his head together.

The casino is large, two levels of gambling along with a shopping and food court downstairs. On a good night we can have close to 25 thousand people in here. Watching the movement of cash is always the main priority so there are two-way windows placed in strategic areas all around. The window in here is to watch the cart as its moved from the northeast quadrant to the counting room. It's here to watch the dealers, and the pit bosses, the floor bosses, and even the waitresses that walk around with free booze. Everyone is always watching everyone here.

"We're short." Pirate's voice is rough.

I turn around quickly, there must be some sort of mistake. "Short? What the fuck are you talking about?"

"Not much just a couple thousand, but enough to throw off the count."

"Fuck, what needs to happen to back track it?" I don't know if it's my military background or what, but my logical brain is always the first to take over in a crisis. If I don't have a plan or know the exact steps needed to get shit done it irks the fuck out of me.

"I need to go through these print outs. It's not going to happen tonight. I've balanced everything out, but I'll look at the numbers and will find out in the next few days whose legs we need to break."

The counter chuckles and we both look at him. He thought we were joking. This wasn't a fucking joke.

"You better hope it doesn't come up as you being the

culprit. I'm not sure you'd enjoy living your life in a wheel-chair, shitting in a diaper." My face is blank as I watch his expression change from slight amusement to fear. There are a few things people know not to fuck with when it comes to the Wings of Diablo—our club, our women, and our fucking money.

Once his head falls back down and he goes back to helping Pirate clear the table up I turn back to the window. There is a commotion at one of the craps tables, I crane my neck to see what's going on. Noting that someone must have won some money, because there is a group of women jumping up and down and laughing. That type of commotion I would allow.

"What the fuck?" I squint my eyes to get a better look at the crowd. Right next to them is a man with an aggressive scowl on his face, an expression I was used to seeing, but next to him was a woman I didn't expect to see.

Isley.

I would know her fucking anywhere even though she was standing there next to that man with about a pound of fucking makeup on her face. There was nothing against the rules about her being in the casino or even gambling. She was nineteen so it was all legal. I just didn't feel right having her here this time of night. Besides, if she was with the piece of shit that was standing next to her it only made me feel more on edge about the whole situation.

"Bro, I'm ready. Let's head out."

"What?" I turn, bumping my head on the glass at the

quick motion. "Shit, yeah. Give me a second. I see someone I need to check on."

"Cool, I'll wait here. Start going through the books." Pirate didn't give me any grief, just pulls up his chair and gets to work.

I walk out of the counting room, walking over to the craps location, but never letting Isley out of my sight. I didn't want to lose her in the crowd. Red flashes in my vision as I watch the fuck standing next to her lean close and point in her face. She cringes as he screams whatever in her ear.

I push my way through guests and workers to get over to her. Though she doesn't even realize I've walked up until I'm standing right in front of her.

"Hold the table." I place my hand up stopping all play. The dealer holds the dice and no bets are allowed to be placed. "What the fuck are you doing here? Where is Christina?"

"Aw man, come on, we're on a roll here." One of the women who had just been celebrating a minute earlier is hopping from foot to foot clearly anxious to keep on playing. I want to tell her to shut the fuck up, but I can't let my reaction to seeing Isley dictate how I treat the players.

"I'm sorry sweetheart, give me one second ok. Those dice will be ready for you in a flash." I shoot her a wink and watch as lust blossoms in her eyes. It doesn't take much for me to get in a woman's pants. I was born in Louisiana. I can turn on that down home charm in a second and have her panties around her ankles.

"Ok, take your time."

"Christina isn't attached to my hip you know." Isley spits out before I can turn away from the woman looking at me like she wants to suck me dry.

"Fine, what are you doing here?" I ask her again.

"I'm on a date." She puts her chin up and stares at me.

"A date, it's nearly three in the morning." I glance at my watch again.

"And I'm a grown woman, Mason."

I don't reply. I can't. I know all too well just how much of a grown woman she has become.

Isley is my little sister's best friend. I've known her most of her life. I remember the exact day I knew that little cry baby Isley had turned into the woman everyone now calls Ice. The day I came home on leave and found her laying on my sister's bed in short shorts, and a cool blue tank top. She hopped out of bed when she saw me in my uniform and jumped in my arms. It was a great homecoming. I had surprised my family, but I was more surprised to see her. Somehow while I was off killing people overseas, she was filling the fuck out and becoming a star player in my spank bank.

"Whatever. Try not to stay out too late if you please. I don't want to hear nothing from Christina tomorrow." I stare at the man standing next to her for a second, but don't acknowledge him. If she didn't feel the need to introduce him, he wasn't that fucking important. I don't know why I'm so tense after that small interaction. It's not like this is the first time I've caught her or my sister for that matter out on dates. Despite that, something about this whole situation makes me feel shitty. I go back into the counting room and wait for Pirate to get his bag. The ride back to the clubhouse isn't more than twenty minutes, but if we really blow it, we could get back in less than fifteen.

"Everything good?" Pirate asks when we finally make it out to the parking lot.

"Yeah, why?"

"Well, you walked back into the counting room like someone had stuck a hot poking rod in your dick." He chuckles at his own joke and secures the crossbody bag with the pick up cash on his body.

"I'm good." I straddle my bike, picking up my lid and get ready to push out.

"You did shit today." a male voice floats in the air and I wait for a second to see who it is. I focus in on him when I realize it's the same bastard that was with Ice in the casino. She is walking alongside him, but as far away as possible it would seem.

"What the hell did you think would happen if I was there? That you would all of a sudden have good luck. I told you that I wasn't good at gambling. This wasn't the best place for a date." She snaps at him.

"Yeah, you did say that, but at least I know you'll make up for it."

"What the fuck is that supposed to mean?" Ice turns in his direction. Just like inside the casino she doesn't even realize that I'm around.

"Yang? What's up? We, good?" Pirate asks from behind me.

I raise my hand, a universal sign I'd picked up in the military that meant to wait.

He goes quiet and waits for whatever is going to happen to play out.

"It means, this was one expensive ass date. I think I'm owed a little in return. I know you agree with that right." The asshole takes a step in her direction and wraps his arms around her waist. The look of absolute shock on her face is apparent even from where I am.

"Tommy you're out of your fucking mind if you think I'm going to sleep with you. Not going to happen. In fact, I want to go home now." She rolls her eyes and turns toward the car they were walking toward. She opens the back door then throws her bag and jacket into the backseat.

"No, bitch. I don't fucking think so." I hear Tommy grunt out as he pushes Isley into the back of the car.

"Tommy! Get the fuck off me! Stop!" I hear Ice scream as she tries to fight him off.

All logic is gone and the savage inside of me takes over. Tommy is a dead man.

CHAPTER

2

YANG

"Tommy, please no! You're hurting me!" Ice screams as the fuck rips at her clothes.

I jump off my bike, and sprint in that direction. I hear Pirate doing the same. I know he's got my back, but based on the way I feel right now I'm not going to need him. I'll be beating the shit out of Tommy all on my own.

I reach him just as he grabs at Ice's shirt and tries to rip it off. I grab the back of his pants and yank him off of her. The motion causing him to tear her shirt. He falls down to the ground completely bewildered by what is going on.

I don't wait for him to say a word. I punch and kick him with everything I have, over and over until I can't hear anything, but my fist slamming into flesh and bone.

"You piece of shit, didn't you hear her fucking say stop. You'll never touch her again. You're going to wish you never fucking met her by the time I get through with you. I stand up tall and bring the heel of my foot down on his dick and I grind it into the ground until I feel his balls pop like soft boiled eggs underneath my foot. He screams out loudly, but this is still not enough pain. He needs to be dead in the fucking ground for putting his fucking hands on Ice.

"Brother! Brother you have to stop! We have an audience." I barely hear what Pirate is saying. It's only when he grabs me up into a bear hug and hauls me off of Tommy that I realize that there are more customers around. They are watching me beat this kid to death.

I suck in deep breaths, wishing for him to get up and say anything to me. "Next time a woman says to get off, you get the fuck off. You limp dick asshole."

"Literally." Pirate laughs as he holds me back.

I had really done a number on him, but he was still alive. Pity.

"I'm good." I put my hands up so Pirate can let me go. "Ice." I turn to find her with her arms wrapped around her chest. The shirt that she had on in tatters. "Fuck, hold on. Are you hurt? I told your ass to go the fuck home! Why didn't you listen?" I bark at her.

"Are you serious right now? I was almost raped and you think telling me I should have gone home is the thing to do? What's next, you going to say I was asking for it, because I had on tight jeans?" She screams in my face and in typical Isley fashion, large tears start falling down her face. I used to tease her mercilessly when she was younger, because the girl could cry at the drop of a hat. No matter the emotion tears would follow—happy tears, sad tears, hurt tears, bored tears. It didn't matter, you could always count on Ice to cry. It took me a long time to realize that it wasn't because she was weak or because someone was getting to her. It was just her body's reaction to the influx of emotion. Nothing more.

"No, fuck. I didn't mean it like that. I'm sorry ok. I didn't mean that. I'm just ..." I exhale and try to get myself under control. She was right. I shouldn't be blaming her for shit right now. This was all this prick's fault not hers. "I'm just on edge. You, ok?" I pull my kutte off and then my shirt. I hand it to her and she stares at me for a second.

"Oh, fuck. Sorry." I stand up out of the car and turn my back so she can have some privacy.

"Alright."

There is a slight bruise on her face, but nothing major that I can see. "Are you hurt? Anything I can't see?"

"No, you got here just in time I guess." She shrugs and wipes the tears off her face. "Thanks for that."

"You don't need to thank me for that. I should have kicked him out when I saw him at the table. I knew something was off about him."

"Brother, I'm going to hit Archer up. We need to stay for the ambulance and the cops. They're going to want state-ments." Pirate says from where he is standing. There is a small crowd and I can see security already working their magic to clear the space.

"Yeah. I know it." I wish I could just take Ice home, but I know she is going to need to stay here and talk to the police. They are going to want to know what happened and she has to press charges. There would be a whole ordeal. Fuck. If only I did this shit where there were no witnesses, I could take his ass out to the swamp and let the fucking gators have him for breakfast. "Listen, Ice maybe you should go on to the hospital. Just let them check you out."

"Mason, I said I was fine. I just want to get back to the dorms."

"You need to at least stay for the police. They are going to want to know why my man here almost beat the hell out of your boyfriend." Pirate speaks up.

"He's not my boyfriend." She spits back.

"Thank God for little miracles." The words are out of my mouth before I can stop them.

"Ugh, just let me know when they get here, please." She glares at me for a second before she hops in the front seat of her car and slams the door shut behind her. I don't have time for her fucking attitude. This shit just added on a few hours to our fucking trip when it should have been a forty-minute trip tops. I should be in my fucking bed right now. Instead, I have to listen to a moaning asshole carry on about how I broke his dick off. Not exactly how I wanted to spend my night.

CHAPTER

3

ICE

I don't know how the fuck I get myself into shit like this. I told Dee that I didn't want to go out with Tommy, but she insisted that I need to loosen up and he was a good guy. His idea of a fun date was to stay out all night in a fucking casino, trying to gamble his fucking life savings away. Then to top that shit off he had the nerve to get jealous, because Mason came over to us. I had more than enough.

"Why the hell do you want to leave already anyway? The night is still young." I open the door that leads to the back parking lot where I'd left my car. Every word that left his mouth just seemed to agitate me more and more.

"It's close to four in the morning. Definitely more of a late middle-aged night." I don't slow down, the sooner I can drop him off the sooner I can get back to the dorms and get this night over with.

"I guess it's for the best anyway, you did shit today."

I cock my head and cut my eyes at him, "What did you think would happen if I were there? That you would all of a sudden have good luck. I told you that I wasn't good at gambling. This wasn't the best place for a date." I had told him when he let me know that we were going to be spending the night in a casino that I wasn't really up for it. I'd never really liked to gamble and had only been in one casino my entire life. It just wasn't my thing. He went on and on about how since I was so new, I would be like a good luck charm for him. Beginner's luck and how he bet I could play anything and come out on top. At the time I thought he was just trying to compliment me and help me out of my shell. Though now it looks like he really thought I was somehow the catalyst he needed to win. How fucking ridiculous is that shit?

"Yeah, you did say that, but at least I know you'll make up for it." He picks up his pace so he can keep up with me. Wait. I'm going to make up for it? What?

"What the fuck is that supposed to mean?" We are right by my car, I hit the small fob on my keys to unlock the doors. I swear to God I just want to leave his arrogant ass here.

"It means, this was one expensive ass date. I think I'm owed a little in return. I know you agree with that right."

My entire body reels as I feel his arm curl around my waist and him push his pelvis in my direction. Eww. What the fuck. If it weren't so nasty that he would even think for a second I would be having sex with him, I would have laughed right in his face.

"Tommy you're out of your fucking mind if you think I'm going to sleep with you. Not going to happen. In fact, I want to go home now." I push him off of me and turn to the back seat. I can't drive with anything on my lap, I always throw my stuff in the back seat. I need to get as comfortable as possible if I'm going to have to deal with his putrid ass all the way back to the dorms.

I wasn't expecting to be hit from behind. I knew Tommy was a jerk, just from the small time I had spent with him tonight. However, I never thought he would attack me.

It's not until my face is roughly forced into the cracked leather of my backseat that I realize what's happening. He flips me over with more force than I can handle.

"No, bitch. I don't fucking think so."

I push at his hands and try to kick him, but he's already crawled on top of me. My adrenaline starts to kick in and I push against him. I'm doing nothing to overpower him. He grabs at my pants and easily pops the button. His breath is hot and smells of the cheap liquor he'd spent most of the night drinking. I can't get a good grip to move him. His pupils are wide and sweat is drenching his hair. If I didn't know any better, I would think he was on drugs. I guess it was the high of becoming a predator. He's going to rape me. I can see that no matter what I say to him right now he is set on taking from me. He grabs hold of my shirt and tries to pull it off, but I angle my arms so he can't before I furiously kick again trying to dislodge him from me.

"Tommy! Get the fuck off me! Stop!" I scream at the top of my lungs, but I know the possibilities of someone being out here this late at night is thin. I should have parked in the main area. This was closer, but it was a bad fucking decision.

He grunts and gets a better grip on my shirt. "Tommy, please no! You're hurting me!"

He pushes a hand hard against my face. My lungs burn as I hyperventilate, scream, and still try to fight him. I was losing my strength fast. I didn't want to give in, but I was about to have no choice.

Just as suddenly as he was on top of me Tommy was being dragged off me and thrown to the ground. The violence of the movement rips my shirt straight down the front.

My entire body shakes and I sit up.

"Mason!" I go to jump out of the car. Only another man, much older than me and bigger, wearing the same vest as Mason stops me.

"Easy there. He needs to do this." The man says and goes back to watching Mason's back.

I have to cover my eyes after a few seconds. Blood is everywhere. Tommy is screaming for mercy and for Mason to stop, but it's like he can't hear anything.

"He's going to kill him!" I say to the man on the side of me. I didn't care about Tommy, but the last thing I want is for Mason to go to jail for this motherfucker. "Please stop him! People are watching."

"You piece of shit, didn't you hear her fucking say stop. You'll never touch her again. You're going to wish you never fucking met her by the time I get through with you." Mason roars out before he picks up his foot and stomps on Tommy's dick. I nearly vomit in my mouth when I see how hard he is pressing down. This was fucking torture.

I tug on the older man's vest and that seems to be key. He grabs Mason and pulls him off Tommy.

The two of them talk for a little while and I do my best to

calm myself down. I only have my bra on and my pants. The shirt that I had on is ripped to shreds. Hell of a fucking night.

I do the breathing exercises I'd learned in my meditation classes. It helps whenever I feel too overwhelmed. Right now, that is exactly how I feel, like it's a sensory overload.

When I open my eyes again, I see Mason leaned over into the car staring right in my face. His dark brown hair is limp and even though it seems like its heavy with sweat it still looks soft. I bunch my hands at my side to keep myself from running my fingers through it.

All the feelings of being overwhelmed seem to disappear the second I look into his light brown eyes. He's always been so strong, a pillar. I can always count on him to bring me a sense of peace. Well, the peace only lasts for a flash this time.

"Fuck, hold on. Are you hurt? I told your ass to go the fuck home! Why didn't you listen?"

I couldn't believe it, was he really blaming me right now. The intense emotions rush back up to the surface and I feel the familiar burn behind my eyelids. I can't stop the tears and I don't even try to anymore. "Are you serious right now? I was almost raped and you think telling me I should have gone home is the thing to do? What next, you going to say I was asking for it, because I had on tight jeans?"

His face falls immediately. I know Mason, I've known him for years. Even though I heard him say the words I knew he didn't mean that. He's not like that.

He spends the next few minutes looking me over and constantly asking me if I'm ok. Now that everything is over, I just want to go home. This whole night was just fucking draining. I knew I couldn't go, because I needed to wait for the police to come. I would tell them exactly what had happened. Tommy should rot in fucking jail for what he'd tried to do to me. Though from the blood pouring out of his face and his crotch I knew I would have to settle for him spending time in the hospital. Mason really did a number on him.

I sit in my car by myself as Mason does his best at damage control. Him and his friends move Tommy away from me and talk with the other people that had come out of the casino. I stare at his back, he wasn't a hulk of a man, but he wasn't thin. He was perfect.

When he was first deployed in the military, Christina was so worried that he wouldn't be ok, because she thought he was too small. I knew different, Mason was just right and a fucking leader to boot. He'd walk in a room and people take notice. I know I did. He was my perfect man.

After about twenty more minutes the police show up and take down my statement. They have to rush Tommy to the hospital. Despite that, the police officers hear from several different people how they saw him on top of me and Mason pulling him off. They take my torn shirt and ask me if I would at least allow them to take pictures of my face and shoulder where there were bruises. I didn't want to go all the way down to the hospital when I had class at 9. I should just ditch, but I was already having a hard time keeping up. I couldn't afford it.

They gave me a card and I promised them that I would come down to the station later to file a report and press charges. Shortly after the commotion came to an end, all that was left in the dark parking lot is a brooding Mason and his friend.

"I'll drive you to the dorms."

"Mason, I'm more than capable of driving. I got my license and everything."

"Isley, I've seen you drive. I'm pretty sure you got your license, because you cried." He smirks at me.

"Forget you. I don't need a babysitter." I flip my hand at him and get myself settled in the driver's seat.

"Go straight to the dorms. I'll check up on you later." He wags his finger at me like I was a fucking child. I hate that shit. No matter what I did or how old I got, I was always a fucking child in his eyes.

"I'm a grown woman, do I have to remind you of that again?"

"Yeah, barely." He scoffs and walks away from me. He and his friend get on their bikes. After sitting there to watch me drive off I see him in my rearview mirror driving in the opposite direction. I didn't want to let him know that I was scared. I had wanted him to come home with me and hold me in his arms like I knew he never would.

CHAPTER 4

YANG

It's nearly five thirty in the morning by the time we make it out from the casino. Archer already knows that there was trouble and is up waiting for us. The last thing that we need right now is someone holding a fucking grudge against us. Adrenaline is slowly starting to drain out of me and I'm starting to feel the toll the night has taken on my body.

I should have made sure that Isley was ok. I should have made sure that she went to the hospital. I should have killed that motherfucker, Tommy. I rev my bike and speed up. I stuff all that extra shit down and focus on what's happening right now. The next step.

Tommy would for sure survive. There is a good chance that when he does come through and he realizes the damage that I've done he will want to press charges against me. I didn't want that fucking legal problem. I would have Bones pay him a little visit before he's able to get out of the hospital.

That would be the same as serving him with a gag order. Bones had a way of getting people to keep fucking quiet.

"Yang, you seeing this shit?"

Pirate's voice sounds in my earpiece.

"What?" I slow down so he can catch up to me. Before he can, I know what he's talking about.

There is a small procession of cars following us. Three. Not the typical Camrys or Accords that people around here tend to drive, but an 85 mustang, 90 thunderbird, and another that was so suped up I couldn't even tell what it was. Whoever was driving these cars loved them.

"What the fuck is this shit? You think they trying to jack us?" I speak calmly to him.

"I don't know. They haven't tried to overtake us and if they know who we are they are dumb as fuck to come back to the clubhouse."

I think on what he just said. What if that is the point? What if they are trying to get us to take them back to the clubhouse? I press my hand to the Bluetooth in my lid and dial the last number.

"Yeah."

"Jam? Who else is on duty with you?" I know what needs to be done and it doesn't involve us taking them to the clubhouse. Either we would have to drive by or we would have to stop and confront the cars behind us. I would feel so much better if we had some back up.

"Shyne and Lex."

"I need you both to hustle the hell up and meet us. We have a tail. I don't want to bring them back to the clubhouse. Seems like that is what they want."

"Heard."

The line ends and I know that Jameson already has backup on the way.

"We keeping it slow?" Pirate asks me.

"Yeah, Jameson is on his way to meet us. As long as they don't start nothing, we can stall them out." I reply. I have to stay on the main road so Jameson can find us, but there are a few ditches and shoulders where we could pull over if we had to.

Just as we bring the bikes down to a torturously slow pace all three of the cars behind us line up and turn on their high beams.

"Fuck, what are they doing?" Pirate hunches down as low as he can to his bike in case anyone starts shooting.

"I don't fucking know." I do the same as Pirate and get low. I want to speed up and get the hell away, but the club-house isn't far. The last thing I want is to bring a problem home. I hear roaring engines and look around for Jameson. What I don't realize is that they have all doubled back and are behind the cars. Now its five against three.

"Yang, you copy?" Jameson locks in on our signal.

"Yeah."

"Park up. Let's see what these bastards want."

I follow orders and ride straight onto the first shoulder. Pirate follows me. The three cars pull to the side and they turn off their engines. Jameson, Shyne, and Lex pull their bikes right behind the cars and they step off. They don't move to come closer to me and Pirate. The idea is to surround them.

Three men get out of the cars. Two of them stand by their

cars, but don't say a word. The third has the nerve to smile and spin in a circle looking at us.

"Is there a reason you are following us?" Pirate asks.

"Yeah, of course there is a reason. I was helping you out." The man in the middle says. He has light skin and is sporting a mohawk, but what really catches my attention is the two large horns that are tattooed on either side of his head.

"Helping us? I didn't know we needed any help?" I turn to Pirate. "Did you call for help?"

"Nah brother."

"See, no one here needs any of the help that you are giving out." I continue.

"That's not what I see. I know that the Wings are carving out a little space for themselves here in NOLA, and I just wanted to let you know that the Drift Demons have your back. We don't ask for much in return."

"Motherfucker, now I know you must be out of your mind. You think we are going to give you something to help us out?" Jameson speaks up from the back. "We don't need that type of help."

"You don't know what you're talking about. You don't know the shit you can get into without the right connections." The man steps forward a few paces getting into Jameson's face which just draws Shyne and Lex closer. If there was going to be any type of fight. They were going to be there to stop it. "I'm Bull by the way." The man with the horn tattoo raises his hand to shake Jameson's, but Jameson doesn't return the gesture. "Oh, It's like that."

"No, but it will be if you don't get the fuck out of my face.

I don't know you and my club doesn't need anything that you are offering."

Bull tsk's and turns back to his car.

"That's a shame. Truly I thought we could be a great team. You may want to talk to your President. Archer may have different feelings about taking on our help. You boys are spread thin and you have a lot of precious cargo to worry about."

"Motherfucker, you know my president? Where the fuck did you come from?" Pirate is the one to step up this time. "That shit sounds like a fucking threat, I say we fucking handle this shit right the hell now."

Bull puts his hands up in mock surrender, "No, this isn't a threat. Just friendly advice. We'll be seeing you boys soon." He gets back into his car and the other two men get back in their cars. They drive off without saying anything. I don't know what they want or who they are, but it sounds like we have new fucking problems to deal with.

CHAPTER

YANG

"What the fuck was that? Have you ever fucking heard of the Drift Demons?"

"No, not once." Shyne says.

"What, are they another MC?" Lex, our newest prospect and Jameson's ol' lady's father asks.

"I don't know, I guess that is what they are trying to be. I'll ask Archer, but this shit is weird as fuck." The ride to the clubhouse is full of questions and paranoia. I do my best to keep everyone focused on the task at hand. Get home in one piece.

We all park our bikes on the side of the clubhouse and walk in. Jameson walks straight to Archer's room and knocks. He may have known that we had problems at the casino, but the Bull character was a whole other level of trouble.

"Church." Archer comes out of his room slipping his shirt over his head. We all follow him in and sit in our designated seats.

"I'm going to need everyone to explain what the fuck

happened in the last three damn hours." Archer looks up to Pirate. "I thought this was a simple pick up."

"It was, I have it right here." Pirate pulls the bag off his body and lays it on the table. There was over 75 thousand dollars in that small duffle bag, not something we should have been riding around with.

"Yang. You tell me what's going on, because I feel like I'm missing something."

"We made the pick up, the books are short, Pirate is going to look into that."

"What the fuck?" Archer shoots him a look and Pirate can do nothing but shrug as I continue to give him the facts of what went down.

"I ran into a family friend, her date decided to get too handsy. I had to deliver a bit of discipline. There were witnesses and cops called. I gave my statement and got the area cleaned up. Once we headed on our way home these Drift Demons started tailing us. I called Jameson for back up. I didn't want to bring them back here. The leader, at least I think he is the leader, Bull says that we need him and his club to give us back up. They want something for it."

"You think this has something to do with the bastard you fucked up back at the casino?" Archer questions.

"No not at all. Tommy is just a college boy who thought he would get away with some shit. This Bull fucker seems like the real deal. I could smell crazy on him, like a bag of wet cats."

"Alright. What are we thinking? I've never heard of the Drift Demons, but according to Jameson it seems like they know of us. Who are we thinking is behind this?" Archer looks around the table for an idea.

"What do you mean what are we thinking? You know what we are thinking. It has to be René." Pirate answers.

"As far as we know, René is fucking dead." Jameson speaks up this time. The raw edge of his voice evident.

"Brother, as much as I would love to agree with you. How the fuck does a dead body just up and fucking vanish? If he was dead when the crew was excavating the site, they would have found his body." Shyne says what we all know.

Jameson's ol' lady tried to sacrificed herself to save her father and to stop the reign of terror René showered over everyone. René had owned and operated one of the biggest underground fighting organizations in all the east coast. Along with that, he was well known in all the criminal circles. He chose Celine as a prize for his son, he had to die for touching Jameson's old lady. We threw a fucking grenade and collapsed a whole fucking tunnel on him. His legs were cut off. Blood caked the walls and dirt. Yet there was no body three days after the altercation.

Jameson believed that someone from his camp came and got him to bury. Others in the club seem to think that René is up and waiting to get his revenge. It's worse than thinking the fucking boogeyman was going to jump out of the damn closet at any second. We didn't have any solid proof either way.

"It's fucking René." Pirate says out loud.

"If it's René then we need to go back into lockdown." Archer leans back in his chair.

"Fuck that."

"We just lifted it."

"How long?"

Everyone starts to complain. No one likes to be on lockdown.

"Now you're complaining? You so fucking set on it being René. We're running from something we don't even know is fucking there. This shit is ridiculous." Jameson grips the edge of the table. He is fighting so hard to not believe that René is still alive. If he is, then his woman and her father were in very real danger. He'd been moody as fuck since we found out, not wanting to leave her alone for even a fucking second. He was possessive before, but if anyone tries to talk to Celine while they are out Jameson is likely to knock them out.

"Hey! Shut the hell up!" I bang my hand on the table. "If our president thinks we need to go into lockdown then that is what happens. His word is law. Though I do agree to an extent with Jameson." I turn to Archer to see if I have permission to voice my opinion. When he nods, I continue. "We don't have any proof that René is alive. This could just be a new player trying to push us out. It could be another MC from further north. Hell, it could be an enemy from one of our many allies. We don't know anything yet. Lockdowns are usually called when we have undeniable proof that the club members and / or our families are in danger." As the Sergeant at Arms, it was my job to know the rules. This was a big one for us.

"Heard." Archer nods his head. He looks away for a second contemplating what we are all telling him right now.

"I won't call lockdown right now. Just know it can happen at any fucking second. I don't want to give anyone any chance to hurt us. You all need to get on fucking board with that. I'll reach out to Wire and Clean to see if they know anything about this crew. Jameson, make sure that everything is squared away at the casino. Pirate, find my fucking money." Archer knocks his knuckles against the table and gets up. A large wave of relief rolls through the members sitting along-side me in church.

I roll my neck from side to side. My muscles are all tense. I'd left the military, because I was sick and tired of always being in a fucking war. All I want is peace and for the past few months it feels like there is always someone around trying to take that from me.

One thing's for sure, I wouldn't be getting any sleep tonight.

CHAPTER 6

ICE

I pull the cover from my head the clock read, 4: 20 PM. I went to the station to file my report , then I made it to my morning classes , but by twelve this afternoon I just couldn't continue. So far, I don't think anyone knew what had happened last night. Christine had tried to ask me about it, but I made up some excuse about being late. I really didn't want to have to rehash everything that went down before I went to my first class.

The door to our private dorm suite opens and I'm so relieved to hear that it's only her and she hadn't brought any other people with her.

"Ice? You here?" She calls out for me.

"Yeah. In my room."

She opens my door and stands at the doorway for a second just glaring at me. She taps her finger against her thigh a few times. Awkward silence fills the room until she starts talking.

"What's wrong?" Her eyes squint like she is staring straight through me.

"Nothing. I'm just tired. I think I'm going to get a few more hours sleep. You going back out?"

"Nope, bullshit. Something is wrong. Do you really think you are going to lie to me and I don't pick up on it? Ice, I've known you since before you could fucking lie. Hell, I basically taught you how to do it. So, I'll ask you again. What's wrong?"

I smirk at her before I let out a deep sigh. There was no way that I would be able to get her to let this go. Christina is just like her brother Mason. The same dark brown hair and light brown eyes, and the same take charge attitude. The only thing that was different was she didn't make constant appearances in my wet dreams.

I grab her face and glue my eyes to hers. "Look I don't want you to freak out, ok? I'm fine. I'm not hurt. Just tired." I had to preface what I was about to say, because she would think the absolute worst before I was even able to finish the story.

"Hurt? What happened?" She hurries and sits down next to me on the bed. "Isley, you better tell me what the fuck happened right now? Do I need to call my brother? Was it Tommy?"

"Hey!" I put my hand up to stop her verbal diarrhea. She would keep jumping to conclusions if I didn't, it didn't help that her conclusions were all correct. "You don't have to call your brother. He already knows and yes it was Tommy. But like I said, I'm fine. Do you hear me? I. Am. Fine." I stare in her eyes making sure that she really hears me.

"I'll be the judge, tell me what happened right now."

I tell her the sordid story starting from the point where Tommy met me at the dorm and suggested that we go to the casino for a date. For the majority of the story, Christina lets me talk. She only adds in the occasional, what the fuck or I'll murder him when I got to any one of the particularly fucked up things Tommy had done or said last night. She became the most animated when I told her that Mason had beat the shit out of Tommy and crushed his balls with the heel of his boot.

"Yeah! That's what I'm talking about big brother! Doing your sister proud!" She claps her hands hard and jumps off the bed, pumping her hand in the air like she'd just won a prize. I laugh at her antics before she sits down and I continue.

"Honestly after that it was all a big waiting game. We had to wait for the ambulance and the police. I'm just worn the hell out." I stifle a yawn for affect.

"I hear you. I'm so happy that he wasn't successful, but babe I don't think you're alright. That shit must have been traumatic as hell. Don't you think you should, I don't know, talk to someone or something like that?"

"Like what? A shrink?" I can't believe she is even suggesting that to me. I've been to several. My parents used to send me to them all the time when I was a kid. They thought all of my crying was due to depression. Several of the quacks had even tried to medicate me for it. I'm just a fucking crier, but no one could understand that. I've always been reluctant to seek that type of help after that ordeal.

"Yeah, why not? I mean just a few times?"

"Why would I do that? I have you." I push her slightly and

she huffs out a breath. "Ok look, I don't think I need it, but if shit starts to get too real. Or I find that I can't deal, I'll go talk to someone."

"Deal." Christina puts out her hand for me to shake. "So, what do you want to do today? You know you're not going to be able to sleep anymore today. You're wide awake"

She knew me like the back of her hand. Once I was up, usually I would stay up. "I know, but it's just my body feels so blah. I'm exhausted." I knew I wouldn't sleep, but that didn't mean I couldn't try.

"How about this? We can order some take out, put on some crappy reality TV and just binge out. No homework, no moving, anything you want."

I scoot over so she could climb in the bed with me. "That sounds like the best fucking idea you've ever had."

"Awesome, let me get the takeout menus." She runs out the room to the kitchen, I hear drawers opening and closing.

I lean back and the images of what happened last night start to replay in my mind. It's so fresh. I feel the tears start to fall down my face. Though I know what Tommy did was fucked up as hell, what I'm focused on is how Mason came to my defense. Things could have been so much worse for me if he wasn't there. I wouldn't be lying here about to enjoy a relaxing night in bed with my best friend. I'd be lying in a hospital bed or even worse in the morgue.

"Fuck, what's wrong? What do you need, tell me." Christina drops the menus on the bed and wraps her arms around me as if she were trying to hold me together.

"I'm fin-"

"If you tell me, you're fine one more time, I'm going to throw you out the window." She pulls me back and glares at me.

"No, honestly, that's why I'm crying. I'm just so damn grateful. I dodged a fucked up bullet thanks to your brother. Tonight could be playing out differently for me if he didn't save me. I'm happy I'm ok." I smile bright at her so she can see that I'm telling the truth.

"True. My brother isn't all the way bad. Guess he gets some cool points for this." She shrugs and rolls over to the other side of the bed. My emotional meltdown disregarded.

We put in an order to our favorite pizza place and lay back watching reruns of Family Guy.

"I guess someone will need to tell Dee that her blind date arranging privileges are revoked."

I scoff and look at Christina like she has three heads, "Ugh, everyone's blind date arranging privileges have been revoked."

"Oh no, Ice, look I know this was bad, but you know not every man is like that. There are some good ones out there. I don't want this to turn you off from everyone." She rubs my thigh trying to console me.

"No, I know that. I just am through searching through the duds. I already know who my good one is." an image of a scowling Mason flashes in my head. He is gorgeous when he smiles, but that pissed scowl he gets when someone is really getting on his nerves is what really turns me on. I have to admit that seeing him beat Tommy up was super scary, but it also turned me on slightly. Fuck, I love it when he loses control like that.

"What? What do you mean you know who your good one is? Who is it?" Christina grabs my arm and shakes me.

"I'm not telling."

"You can't be serious."

"I am, I need to do this on my own time. I don't want you pressuring me, I won't tell." I sit up in the bed and cross my legs underneath myself.

"But I'm your best friend!" She whines.

"You are and I love you, but this secret stays with me." I chuckle.

"Fine, can I at least talk about him? Like why the hell aren't you with him?"

"Oh, he just sees me as a friend, I'm sure. Neither one of us has ever taken a step in that direction, you know? He doesn't even look at me in that way." I try to stay as vague as possible I didn't want to tip her off to the fact that I was talking about her brother.

"Yeah right. He's feeling you."

I toss my head back and laugh hard, "How the hell can you say that? You don't even know him."

"Ice, you are fucking gorgeous and single, no major character flaws. He'd be crazy if he didn't, I mean he's not related to you or anything like that right?"

"Eww, no."

"Then he's feeling you." She picks up a slice of pizza, proceeds to pluck off the pepperoni and put it in her mouth.

"I don't know how to take the next step. I've waited for a

while, he's never going to do it. I don't know how to get the hell out of the friend zone." Or the little sister's friend zone.

"I know this is probably going to go against everything you stand for, but just fucking do it. Take charge. Let him know that you want him and then take him."

"You talk like he's a slice of pizza or something like that. I can't just take him. What if he doesn't want me?" I twist a thread coming off my blanket around my index finger trying to find something to do with this nervous energy building up inside of me. If I didn't do something I would start to cry again.

"We already had this conversation. Is he related to you? No, right? Then he wants you."

I sigh and fall back onto the bed.

"Ok, a better plan." She grabs my hands and pulls me back up into a sitting position. "Seduce him. Wear some sexiness. Tempt him. Throw yourself at him without letting him know you really like him, if he takes the bait go for it. If he still ignores you, then you know."

I think about that plan and even though I know I would be so fucking uncomfortable it could work. In all the time that I've known Mason I've had a crush on him. When I was younger I would for sure classify it as a schoolgirl crush. I wrote his name alongside mine in my diary, played MASH with only his name in the spouse section. But as I got older, the schoolgirl crush legit blossomed into love.

I'd never so much as kissed Mason and I was in love with him. The problem is he is nine years older than me and for a large part of my childhood he was back and forth in the military. I'd never even gotten the chance to flirt with him. I was always pining for him from afar. The time for loving him from afar had passed. He is my ideal man, I want him, and I'm all grown up. Christina thinks I should tempt him, offer him something that he can't resist and see if he reacts. I have just the thing—my virginity.

"That sounds like a good idea. Tell me how I seduce him."

Christina's eyes open wide when she realizes I'm serious. She claps and launches straight into techniques. I do my best to pay attention to what she is saying, but all I can think about is how I'm going to finally have what I've always known to be mine. I've waited to give myself to Mason, but I'm tired of waiting for him to realize what I can be for him. Time for me to go for what I want. Mason is not going to know what hit him.

CHAPTER 7

YANG

It's been about a week since Bull and his boys made their appearance. We hadn't seen or heard anything from them. Bones made sure that Tommy was quiet about what had happened that night. I checked on Christina and Ice the day after the incident. Everything seems like it is moving along well, but I'm still having such a hard time shaking that night out of my mind. It robs me of my calm. My peace. I hate feeling like this.

Loud cackling laughter draws me out of my room and into the main area.

"Why are you always here? It's like fucking home all over again. Go away!" Shyne grumbles at Tink who seems to be making more and more appearances at the club. Celine and her have quickly become inseparable. Shyne likes to throw digs at her, but he doesn't truly mean it when he says that he wants her to go away. I know he feels better with her in the clubhouse than out on her own.

"I hope it's not. I couldn't stand going over to your house

and watching you play world of warcraft with your strange orc friends."

"Oh ... fuck you ..." Shyne's mouth drops open and he literally storms away.

"No! He was one of those WOW groupies?" I didn't usually get in on their conversations, but I had to get in on this one. It was too good not too.

"Was? I'm sure that if we look real hard, we could find it on one of his computers. That shit took up hours of his time."

"Get out!" Shyne screams from his room.

For the first time in about week, I laugh big hearty belly laughs. "Are you serious?" I just can't believe it. By the time I finish up laughing I'm crying and holding my gut. This shit will never go away. It's going to be my happy place for a while.

"Oh, by the way Yang, Luke said it was ok for a few of my girlfriends to come over. We want to have a little bonfire outside, just the girls." Daria walks over to me and entwines her arm with mine.

As the ol' lady to the president there was really nothing that she could do that I would be able to say no to, especially if it were already approved.

"Oh cool. I'll invite a few people too." Tink pipes in.

"Alright, a few people. That's fine." I don't see Celine out here with Tink and Daria. It's not strange as of recently. Jameson must have her fucking locked in the room with him. We've all been trying to get him to loosen up the reins when it comes to her. It's starting to feel like the woman is more prisoner than his girlfriend.

I knock on his door and sure enough Celine is on the bed reading a book and Jameson is on his computer.

"Celine, you know Tink is here, right?" I say with my head poked in.

"Really? Yay!" She drops the book and nearly runs me over trying to get out.

I have to back all the way up to stop myself from falling over. When I look back to Jameson, he has a scowl on his face and his leg is bouncing up and down.

"Bro, where you at?"

"What?" His attention is squarely on me now, "What the fuck are you going on about now?"

"Jameson, you're suffocating the shit out of her. You're going to lose her and not to René or whatever other bastard tries to come in here and take her. She is going to run away on her own."

He jumps out of his seat, his hands already balled into fists. "She's not fucking going anywhere. Celine wouldn't leave me."

"She doesn't want to, that I'm sure of, but you're not really giving her too much of a choice here. You knew Tink was here, didn't you?"

When he looks away, I know that he did.

"Why you got her sitting in here like a grounded child then? You guys hardly ever go out. You don't do anything that requires you to be away from her for very long if you don't absolutely have to and she never sees any of her friends or does anything on her own. What the fuck do you think is going to happen if you let her loose a bit?"

"One of René's fucking goons kidnap her! Anyone for fuck's sake." Jameson harshly answers.

"Yeah, that's all a possibility. But it's also a possibility that they walk in here and just rip her out of your arms. It's a small possibility, but that shit could happen too. Listen to me, " I put a hand on his shoulder, I'm ready to get out of his space. He's so fucking tense it feels like the emotion is leaking onto me. "Let her have some fun now, because it might be a while until she does again."

"Fuck, alright. I hear you."

Jameson runs his hands through his hair and takes a few steps back. The anger already dropping out of his stance. "You want to help me in the back shed. I want to take a few things out. Hobby pieces for Lex."

"Aww, sucking up to the father-in-law." I tease him.

"Shut up." Jameson walks by me and I follow behind him.

The girls are all cackling by the small bar area. I see Daria on the phone probably to let her friends know that it's okay for them to come over. It'll be nice to have a few people over. Have some fun.

Two hours later and we have a large portion of the back shed sectioned off and set up for Lex. Lex is a great boxer, but with the damage done to his hands he'll never be able to do that professionally again. Apparently, he'd told Jameson how carpentry was the one thing he really missed doing. Except he knew that he would never have the space or the equipment to really get back into it. Jameson went out of his way to get the starter shit for him. He may be Lex's superior when it comes to the club, but the man was still his woman's father. There would always be a different level of respect there. Most of the shit that he needed was hard to fucking move and by the time we had finished it all I was dripping sweat.

"This asshole better use every last piece of this shit." Jameson leans against one of the beams in the shed. He's breathing just as hard as I am.

"You got that shit right. Next time get the prospects to do this shit. I don't think I need to work out for the rest of the fucking week." I pull my arms over my head and stretch out the aching muscles.

"Yeah right, you know that shit isn't going to fly with Archer."

"Man, yeah. I know." Archer and Jameson were in the same unit in the military, so he knows exactly how much of a control freak Archer is. One of the wonderful activities that Archer had brought back with him from the military is the physical exercise. In the beginning, he would be outside by himself exercising first thing in the morning. Then shortly after the club was fully on its feet, Shyne started going out there with him and they would work out together. After that it was Jameson and me. Within a week everyone including Pirate was out there with him. After three weeks of all of us doing this, Archer had made it mandatory. Something about being fit made us better riders. Had no fucking idea who the fuck had told him that shit. I didn't really mind and he wasn't a hard ass about it if one of us really didn't want to come out.

Though I knew my muscles would be aching even worse the next time we had to exercise.

"I can't wait to get in the fucking shower."

"Fuck man me too." Jameson and I walk out of the shed, satisfied with what we had done with the space and began to walk back over to the clubhouse.

"What the fuck is this?" Jameson's voice is cold and hard. He's pissed and I feel the same way.

Cars were lining the front of the clubhouse. Not one or two, but at least five that I could see. "Didn't they say it was going to be a few girlfriends. It looks like they had invited the whole fucking town." I grumble out before I pick up the pace towards the clubhouse.

"You don't think it's Bull, do you?"

"No, these cars look like shit. Relax man." I do my best to ease his mind, I would be lying if I said that same thought hadn't crossed my mind though. The only assurance I had was that people were still walking in and there were no gunshots.

"I'm going to fucking kill Tink. She knows better than to do this shit." I hustle to the clubhouse. Having a few people over was fine. When it became dozens, it was a goddamn problem. There was no way for us to secure everything even when we had notice. This impromptu shit was enough to get someone hurt.

Jameson is right behind me every step of the way. I'd told him it wasn't Bull and his crew, but I don't think he will believe me until he sees it for himself. This would be his worst fucking nightmare.

I burst in the door and see a prospect working hard to bring out the extra bottles of booze from the storage room.

"Tink!" I call out to her. She is standing near the back corner of the clubhouse trying to get the DJ equipment set up. Shyne is there next to her. They are in a heated debate and I can only assume that he is telling her the same shit that I'm about to ream her out for.

"Who the fuck is paying for all this shit, because this isn't a club thrown party. You fucking overstepped Tink. This shit isn't ok."

"What do you mean, Daria said it was ok for us to invite people."

"Yeah, a few, you invited every damn body you know!" Shyne screams at his cousin.

I need to know what was going on right the hell now. I step in between the two of them. "Tink, what did you do?"

"Oh God, you going to get on my case too? This jerk and Bones already did that. I thought it was ok. I've already invited everyone and the bulk of the party goers should be here already. I didn't do it to just be hardheaded. I thought we were having fun."

A small lightbulb goes off in my head. This might be the last time we are able to throw a party. Archer did tell us that we may need to go on lockdown at a minute's notice. It's completely against the rules to have a party of this magnitude without securing everything. Although if this was the last time that we were going to be able to do it than maybe this was ok.

"Everyone over eighteen?"

"What? Are you serious? You're good with this?" Shyne asks completely confused. It's my job to make sure the rules are upheld; this was a clear breach.

"I'm not good with it, but it may be just what we need. You heard Archer, when is the next time we are going to be able to throw a party? We may all be stuck behind these walls with no contact to the outside very soon."

"Yes. Everyone is over eighteen. I'll even get some of my responsible friends to man the bar and make sure they don't serve anyone under twenty-one booze."

"Nah, that's what we have prospects for." I scratch a hand over the scruff on my face. "I need to get up with Archer and double check everything maybe we can get a few bunnies here and make it official."

"Sounds like you need a bit of release." Shyne speaks up.

"Yeah, it's been a bit." I shake it off and get to business. "Listen, get shit set up the best that you can let me go check in with Archer."

I leave them all and walk toward Archers room. I knock, but don't hear anything coming from the other side. I don't want to just barge in. I knock again and then the door is ripped open, startling me.

Archer is standing there, fury plastered all over his face. When I look inside, Daria is standing with her head down and her hands fumbling by her lap. He must be screaming on her too. Shit these girls were really being put through it today.

"What?" Archer barks at me.

"I want to talk to you about this party."

"I know this shit is fucked up. I'm already talking to her about it."

It's not my place, Archer is the president. Only now that I'm thinking about it, I feel like this might be a really good idea. "Can I give my opinion?"

He squints at me, unsure of what more I would have to say, "You don't want to find the quickest way to get everyone the fuck out of here?"

"No."

His eyes pop open and he backs out of the doorway for me to come in. "Go on."

"Ok, here's my thought, them just inviting people we don't know is completely a security breach. But on the same note, with everything that is going on this might just be what everyone needs."

"How you figure that?"

"Archer, honestly when is the next time we are going to be able to have a party? When will we know for sure that we won't need to go into lockdown? Just the same way it doesn't give us a lot of time to prepare the clubhouse, it doesn't give the enemy a lot of time to plan to attack us. This spontaneous event might be the only way we are able to have a good time right now. We all need it. Jameson is about to drive himself crazy worrying about Celine. Pirate is becoming paranoid as fuck and I've been on edge all fucking week. Letting loose for a little bit can put all that to rest even for a little while. Though whatever you think is best I'll run with. I can get the clubhouse cleared within the next fifteen minutes if you want." I stand back and wait for Archer to deliver his orders.

It would take a few minutes. If there is one thing about Archer I know, he's fair and logical. He may blow off the handle, but if you can get him to hear you out, he will really think about what needs to be done.

He nods to me, but before he says a word he walks over to his wife and lifts her head. She hadn't moved an inch since I came in the room. I know they have a D/s relationship though I don't know exactly what that entails. She is very obedient most of the time. He plants a soft kiss against her lips and caresses her face. I can't hear what he is saying to her, but I'm thinking its somewhere along the lines of I'm sorry. Her entire body relaxes as she wraps an arm around his neck. They kiss for a second before he comes back over to where I am.

"You're right, this may be the last time that something like this can happen. I want this compound as secure as possible in the next few minutes, at least before we are overcrowded. Get everyone moving."

"Copy. Speaking of everyone, can I invite some bunnies."

"Yeah, get them over here."

I nod and turn to walk out of the room. Now that I knew what the next steps were, I could see the clear path to making sure that we all had a good time.

Finally, tonight I would be able to shake this shit off and get back to what I normally feel like. Who knows maybe I would find a sweet honey hole for me to fall into. I smile just thinking about it. If this was going to be the last time we were going to be able to party hard, I wanted to make sure I got my fill.

CHAPTER

YANG

Within an hour and a half the entire club is packed—friends from in town, the bunnies, some coeds from the university. Capri even came over to help us bartend. It was turning into a full blown rager and it was having the exact effect that I thought it would have. All the members were having a good time. Jameson and Bones were arguing over a pool game between the two of them. The dancers were all in rare form, doing tricks on the moveable stages. I took another drink and just smiled at how quickly the vibe of a place can change. Good music and family will do that to you.

"Yang!" Tink runs over to me and instantly I'm on edge. It's not until I see the smile on her face that I relax. "You have to come see this craziness." She grabs my hand and pulls me to the back of the clubhouse.

"Wait! Where are we going? Who is going to keep guard?"

"Yang, it's a party. Besides, Jameson and Bones are right there. Clay is at the door. We're good." She continues to pull me out the back doors. There is a large crowd and again my hackles go up.

"I'm giving 3 to 1 on Snapper here." Lex stands up on something and starts looking around the crowd. People rush him with money.

"What the hell is this?" I push my way through the crowd and can see Archer and Shyne laughing like crazy people. Pirate is standing there next to Lex with a notepad in his hands.

In the center of the crowd is two women in what I think are bikinis standing in what looks like a man-made mud pit. They are in their bras and underwear. Both of them are smiling, moving back and forth like they are getting ready to fight.

"These dumb bastards decided today was a good day to have a mud wrestling competition." Tink says from behind me.

I look from her to the women in the middle to Archer who was laughing so hard there were tears coming out of his eyes. Celine was talking to one of the girls and Daria was talking with Pirate pointing people out. This is fucking gold.

"Fuck yes. Tell them to hold up. What's the bet?"

"Shanel, who they've been calling Snapper has 3 to 1 odds. I look at the girl. I don't know if she has any fighting ability, but she does look like she is in good shape. The other seems to be smaller, but there is a confidence in her eyes that I recognize.

"Put me down for twenty on that one."

"Justine?"

"That's her name?"

"Yeah, but she's so small." Tink frowns a bit.

I smile at her, "Don't you know the saying ... It's not the dog in the fight, but the fight in the dog!" I back track from her. Jameson and Bones will be pissed the hell off if they miss this shit. "Tell them to hold it until I come back with the rest of the guys."

Tink nods and I rush into the clubhouse to find the two of them. Jameson sees me moving fast in his direction and the smile he just had drops off his face. Of course, he thinks that something is wrong.

"It's good, we're good. You motherfuckers are about to miss the main fucking event outside." I say the second I get close enough.

"What the hell is happening outside?" Bones questions.

"Trust me the game can wait."

They both put their pool sticks down and follow me out to where the mud fight is about to go down.

"No, you can't be serious." Bones puts a hand over his mouth like he's about to be emotional. "Is this for me, because this might just be the best day of my life."

Jameson laughs once he realizes what is going on and goes over to help Pirate and Daria. It's a fucking blast to watch the two girls wrestle and throw each other around in the mud. Justine wins the first fight and just as I thought it was over two other girls volunteered to fight. The last fight was between Celine and Puff, one of the club bunnies. Of course, Jameson didn't let her fight in her underwear. I could have told Puff that she had no shot against Celine. The girl might not have been a professional, but she was a trained fighter.

It didn't take her but four moves to pin Puff. The bunny argued that it was unfair, but we all saw it. Thankfully, I don't think anyone actually bet on Celine to lose, no one was that stupid. By the end of the fights the crowd on the inside of the compound was still having a great time. The music was blaring, and everyone was just at ease.

"Yang, you want to spend some time with me today or are you going to pretend I don't exist again?" I wasn't expecting to be cornered the second I walk back into the clubhouse. Yet that is exactly what happens and it's by one of the club bunnies that I haven't had the pleasure of being with.

"Twig, I told you before I wasn't ignoring you, I just didn't have time."

"Seems like you're free now." She runs her hand up my chest. Twig is a pretty girl, she's in her late twenties and maybe a bit jaded by her profession, but she's nice to look at. I don't know why I can't bring myself to fuck her. Something about her just turns me off. I don't know if it's the condescending way she looks at some of the other girls or the fact that she needs to have her way no matter what. Though I've never actually felt like I was missing out whenever I had missed the chance to plow into her.

"No, don't think so. Why don't you check with Pirate he's in a good mood?" I squeeze her arm and step around her. I want to go upstairs and wash my hands right away. I had some mud on my pants and my shirt. I need to get out of these dirty clothes and come back down to enjoy the party.

By ten at night the party was starting to die down which was just fine with me. Less likely for anything crazy to happen. I walk over to the bar and get a drink from Capri. "This shit is off the hook!"

She yells at me over the music as she pours a double shot of Jack Daniels for me.

"Off the hook?" I shake my head.

"Don't shake your head. You're not that old." She laughs.

"Yeah, but you are." I pull out a tip for her and slide it across the bar.

"This was the right fucking thing to do." Archer sits down at the stool next to me.

"Yeah, I think so too.

Archer and I sit there for a long while and just talk shit. Both of us are enjoying the down time. Daria is the one to break up our little bro time when she wraps her arms around him and snuggles into his back.

"Ma chérie."

"Luke, you're ignoring me." She speaks directly into his ear, but it's loud enough that I hear it.

I turn away from them, some things are just not meant for my eyes. What I see on the other side of the bar forces me to do a double take. Ice is sitting there with a drink in front of her and about a pound of makeup on her face. I wipe my eyes thinking maybe I've had a bit too much to drink, but when I look again, she's still there. She sees me watching her and gives me a smile, but a man walks up to her and starts chatting her ear off. Her attention is now on him.

I don't want to cause Capri any fucking grief, but I know for a fact that Ice shouldn't be drinking. Yet there she is with a damn drink in her face. I watch Ice and the man talk for a few moments before I force myself to look away. Isley is a big girl. I would have expected her to take a little time off before she started dating again, but I'm not going to judge her for it.

I get another drink and contemplate going to my room for the night. The carefree mood I had just a second ago is gone and now I'm back to feeling tense. I hear Ice's tinkling laugh over the music and curse myself for letting her get to me.

What the hell is she doing here? Why isn't she at the dorms? Who the fuck is that man she is talking to?

I roll my neck from side to side and contemplate finding Twig to see if she's free for the night. That only gets me more pissed, I don't want Twig. What I want I can't have.

Isley is way too young. She is barely nineteen and my little sister's best friend. I've known her for years and fucking her should be the last thing that is on my mind right now. I pound back another drink trying to purge her from my mind. When I glance back in her direction, I don't see either one of them.

"Fuck, where the hell did she go?" I scan the crowd, praying that the jerk didn't do anything that I would have to kill him for. We like to send all of our guests home in one piece. There has been a time or two where that wasn't a possibility though.

I drag my gaze over to the other side of the bar thinking maybe she somehow got around me that way. When I still don't see her, I dig in my pocket and pull out my phone. I would have to get my little sister to give me Isley's phone number. I need to make sure she is alright and able to get back to the dorm rooms ok. If she was drinking, I didn't think it was safe for her to drive. Fuck I can't drive either. I've had quite a few drinks back to back, I'm only a drink and a half away from sloshed.

"This seat taken?"

My head snaps to the left and I see Ice leaning against the seat that Archer had left open. Her cold blue eyes stare straight into mine. The dark mascara on her lashes making her eyes seem even lighter than they usually are. Her mouth is a pinkish colored and her long hair is ironed pin straight. I prefer her more natural look, but I can get into this as well. "Well, are you going to let me sit here with you?" She tilts her head to the side and waits for me to answer.

I should tell her no. Fuck, it.

CHAPTER

9

ICE

I can't believe he hasn't come over to talk to me yet. Every-thing about Mason is hard. I sip on my drink not wanting anyone to think I'm sitting here at a party solely waiting for one of the members to take notice of me. Only I must not be doing a good enough job, because a random man comes over to me and tries to start a conversation.

"You here with someone?"

"Excuse me?" I lean back so the man isn't so in my space. After Tommy, I'm wary of anyone getting too close to me.

"Do you have a boyfriend or something like that?" He leans even closer and screams in my ear.

"No, I'm here with some friends." I answer, it was a half-truth. Tink had called Christina and told her that they were throwing a party here. Of course, she didn't want to come to the party, but I made up an excuse about inviting my secret friend. She thought this was the greatest place for me to make my move. She took her time primping and dolling me up. I look more like a slut than I ever have in my life, though according to most people that didn't take much. Apparently, I have a very sexual face. I don't know how that's possible. I've had a few men say that my resting face is sultry. One went so far as to say I had come fuck me written in my eyes. I laughed in his face and then kicked him out of my life. Besides the fact that I have always been hung up on Mason, none of the boys my age were ever mature enough for me to even think about having sex with them. Mason may have been the only one that has ever just looked at me like I was a person. Today I would try to get him to look at me like I was the porn star of his dreams. If only I knew how to do that.

"Did you hear me?" The man that had somehow made his way into my space again says. I had completely blocked him out. I'm too nervous thinking about how I'm going to get Mason to notice me. I was already batting zero. According to Christina if I give a man the come hither look, they are supposed to fucking come hither. Mason did not.

"Oh no, I'm sorry. I zoned out. I'm not really feeling it tonight, I'm going to find my friends and get out of here." I politely smile and wait for him to move so I can get up.

"Aw, that sucks. I was really hoping to get to know you a little better." He tries to charm me, but his eyes have ping ponged between my breasts so much that I know exactly what he wants to get to know better.

"Sorry, maybe next time." I move my legs, forcing him to get out of my way or get hit. I look over to where Mason is and see that he is still in the same spot, but his jaw is locked and tense. That sexy ass scowl is on his face.

Ok, you can do this. The worst thing that can happen is he says no. He probably will.

My stomach flips as I think about him telling me no. I would never be able to face him again after tonight if he laughed me away.

No, don't think about that. Just know that the worst-case scenario is a little embarrassment. Best case is you have the man of your dreams rocking your world tonight.

My inner vixen moans at that thought, a long needy sigh leaving her mouth.

I try to channel her as I walk around crowd leaving the man who I turned down at the bar and make my way to where Mason is. The clubhouse is so packed that I have to move in a large arch in order to find enough space to walk. As I come up behind him, I see him stand up on the pegs of his stool and look around. I don't know what he's looking for, but I move a little faster in case he is thinking about getting up and leaving. This is my only shot. I reach him just as he sits back down and pulls out his phone.

What do they say in all the movies, "This seat taken?"

The shock on his face when he turns and sees me makes me feel like maybe he didn't recognize me across the bar. He stares at me for a second, the scowl on his face deepening and his gaze on me getting a bit uncomfortable. "Well, are you going to let me sit here with you?"

"Go for it." He finally says.

"Thanks, this is an awesome party." I lean close to him and speak in his ear. When I sit back, I pull my glass up to my mouth and take another sip. At least I try to, Mason takes it away before the liquid can touch my perfect mauve lips.

"Yeah, an awesome party you shouldn't be at. You know

you're not supposed to be fucking drinking. You're too young for that shit." He ranted.

Here we go with the too young shit, "Mason. It's fucking soda. For Christ's sake." I glare at him. He squints his eyes and takes a sip of my drink. His mouth on the same space mine just was. He shrugs and slides my cup back to me. "Besides, I've been taking drinks for a few years now. I think I can handle myself." In a bold yet normal move I reach over and take his cup to toss back the liquor in there. I don't even wince as the liquid sizzles down my throat and into my stomach.

"Hmm, whatever, I'm not holding your hair if you get pissy drunk."

I raise an eyebrow at him, he's lying. He's already held my hair back before when I threw up. Instead of booze I had a stomach virus and was sick at their house. He calls the bartender over and orders another drink for himself before looking at me, "You want another?"

"Sure!" I say not trying to sound too excited.

He signals to the bartender for another shot, but she gives me a strange look. She must know that I'm not old enough to be drinking. He puts his hand out and signals for the bottle. Just like that with no push back she hands it over. Must be nice to be so fucking powerful. She gives him another glass and he pours the both of us a shot. I don't shoot mine right away. The last thing I need right now is to get drunk. He isn't on the same page with me, he drinks his right away and then pours another.

"What are you doing here Ice?"

"The same thing everyone else is doing, partying." I laugh and tap his thigh with my hand. He tenses for a second before he relaxes again and takes another drink. I didn't think it would be so hard to talk to him. I know a lot about him, but what I didn't know about was this club. This was one part of his life that he kept mostly secret from his sister. She knew that if there were ever any trouble no matter what that they would do their best to take care of it, but not the ins and outs. Christina didn't know about any of that.

"So, what does this mean?" I rub my hand over the patches on his vest.

"What does what mean?" He screams back in my ear.

"The patches … What's an SAA? Yang?" I have to lean in close to talk to him. The music is loud and it's hard to have a meaningful conversation screaming at one another.

"Yang, is my road name." He yells.

"Why?" I stay close against him waiting for his answer, but also making sure to lean my breast against his arm. It's innocent enough, but it feels so fucking good.

He opens his mouth to talk and starts yelling again. A new song comes from the small DJ booth and it's almost impossible to hear over it.

I move back and shake my head no. "Mason, don't you stay here? Where is your room. All this music is giving me a headache." I rub a finger to my temple. Another tip from his sister. Do what you have to do to get him alone. According to her if he didn't want to then that was the first indicator that he didn't want me. If Yang told me to go home or that he didn't want me in his room I'd abort the whole fucking mission.

He opens his mouth, but doesn't say anything. Instead, he grabs the bottle, his cup, and my hand, and he pulls me towards what I'm guessing is his room. This is nothing new. I'd been in his room before, of course that was when I was ten and he just got the new Xbox. A tall man, beelines straight for us. On his vest was the name Jameson and under it another patch that said VP. I wonder if that meant he was more important than Mason. When he was close enough Jameson flung out his arms and planted his hand right in the middle of Mason's chest stopping us in our tracks. The man looks me up and down before settling on my face. I'm in a dark silver bodycon dress and have on killer red and silver heels. I'm only five foot five inches, but with the heels I'm about five nine. I don't understand why he's stopped us until he leans forward and blurts out one word loud enough for both me and Mason to hear.

"Age?"

"She's nineteen. Yes, I know that for sure, family friend. Besides we're not going to fuck." Mason yells back. My heart falls slightly. That is exactly what I'd wanted to do.

Jameson raises one eyebrow at him, but walks off. He was just making sure that I wasn't going to cause any trouble. I can appreciate friends like that. Mason starts walking again and we finally make it into what I'm assuming is his room. It's not very big, a little junky, but nothing that would cause me to turn and walk out. He has a small love seat on the side of the room. He walks over and gathers up the clothes that are lying there. I close the door behind me and instantly It's like I can hear myself think. I didn't even realize just how loud it was out there.

"Geez, I'm surprised I still have eardrums." I joke and sit down where he'd cleaned off the small sofa.

"Yeah, our parties are usually much bigger than this." He sits down next to me, but not thigh to thigh. Instead, he sits with his back to the armrest and one of his legs folded up on the couch creating as much space as possible between us. So much for getting closer in here.

"Yeah, I've been to one before today. This is much milder than that one." I didn't want there to be a lull, so I went back into questioning him about his club. "Yang? Why Yang?"

"The boys seem to think I bring a certain peace to the club-house." He answers.

"Ah, I get it. That's cool. I agree." I pick up my glass and take a small sip.

"I don't … not recently." He pours himself another drink and takes a big gulp.

"Why? Something happen recently? You've always been incredibly easy going even when bad shit was going on, you were always the one to see the best in it."

He chuckles and puts the bottle of jack down on the floor, "Yeah that was years ago. I've done a lot of growing up since then."

"Nah, I don't think so. I think that is just more of who you are. That's not something that is going to change. If there is something throwing off your vibe, maybe you need to

63

address it instead of just accepting that this is your new normal."

He leans back further into the arm of the loveseat. "Look who the fuck got her psychology degree. Shall I lay flat on the couch so you can diagnose all my problems." He pokes fun at me and I punch him in the chest. Definitely not sexy, but it was us. This was easier. The words seemed to flow now that I stopped focusing on how I could be ultra sexy and just be me. I don't know how long we stay in the room and talk, but by the time the conversation stops flowing naturally, my shoes are off, my hair is pinned back, and I don't hear anything going on outside.

"You drunk?" Mason asks.

"Nah, I'm good why?"

"It's late. I can't drive you back to the dorms, but I could call a cab for you." He yawns once and pulls out his phone.

Crap, I'd wasted too much time, "No wait, don't call the cab yet. I don't need it." I put my hand over his, so he stops. "Besides, it's not that late. You can't hang anymore?"

"Hang?" He crosses his arms over his chest, his eyes boring into mine. "Ice, what are you doing here? I thought you came to party. The party is over."

Ok Ice, it's time to gut up.

"Well, I did come to party, but I really came to see you."

"Yeah? For what?"

"I wanted to come over and tell you how grateful I am for everything that you did for me. That shit could have been so bad. Much worse."

"Yeah, it could have. I hope you picked a better one this time around."

What? This time around? "A better one?"

"Yeah, I saw you at the bar with that kid. Is he your boyfriend?"

I chuckle and roll my eyes. "Oh please, I didn't even know who he was. Besides, he was too concerned with trying to monitor my breathing. I don't think his eyes ever left my chest."

"Fuck? Really? I knew I should have fucked him up." He looks away, the closed off position he was just in dropped.

"You'd have to fuck everyone up."

"I could do that." His face tells me he's serious. He would beat everyone up for me. That's just how he is.

Time for the big guns. This is it. "No matter how many people you beat up it's never going to change the fact that most men if not all of them are scumbags. I'm tired of waiting on someone to show me that they're not an asshole. Feels like it's never going to happen. Once they get a look at me all they see is which way they want to fuck me. Then when they figure out I'm still a virgin ..."

"Wait, still?" Mason jerks forward.

"Yup, I'm still carrying this dumb ass V card. if I could find at least one person who wasn't a complete jerk I'd do it, but so far I've only met one who fits the bill."

"Oh, yeah?" He leans back, the beginnings of a scowl on his face. "Good for him. You should go get him then."

"What do you think I've been trying to do all night?" My voice is soft, but I keep my gaze locked on him.

He blinks a few times and his eyebrows knit together before he looks from side to side like he's missing something. "Isley, what the fuck are you talking about?"

"Just hear me out, ok?"

"I don't think I want to hear this shit. You got to go." He goes to stand up, but I put my hand on his thigh to stop him.

"Mason, just wait ok. Listen to me. This is not just some drunk mistake. I've thought about this. I'm not intoxicated. I'm not rushing into anything." I lean back and do my best to sell him on taking my virginity. "I know you, Mason. I know pretty much everything about you."

"No, you don't. You just know what my sister tells you. That is what you know." He snaps at me. Fuck this may not have been a good Idea. I want to walk out, but I refuse to give up now that I'm so close.

"Fine, even so, I know enough about you to know that you're the best choice. All my friends say that losing your virginity is not that big a deal, but I know that's bullshit. That shit is going to stay with me forever. What better way to lose it than to someone I know is a good man and isn't just trying to get another notch on his bedpost. I trust you, Mason. I know you'd never hurt me. That is all I'm asking for. I want you to take my virginity so in thirty years when I look back, I know I didn't lose it to some phony asshole in the back of his truck. But to someone I knew was a good guy and who truly cared for me in some capacity."

"Isley ..." he turns himself on the couch, so he is sitting the right way. He leans forward and puts his hands on his head. "We can't do this. You're my little sister's-"

I was so fucking tired of that shit, "I'm Isley, Mason. I'm not your sister. I'm not a little kid. I'm a grown woman who knows what I want and I'm asking for it."

"Fine, but you should be with someone your age. I'm almost ten years older than you. You need to find someone who will wine and dine you, woo you, shit like that."

"Mason, really?" I giggle then get up from where I'm sitting. I kneel in front of him in between his knees and sit back on my ankles. "You've dined me more than any man in my life. I've drunk with you. I respect you. I have fun with you. I can depend on you. As for the wooing ... We are in the 21st century, boys my age don't do that shit. The best wooing I would ever get is someone offering to buy me a slushie from the cafeteria." We both chuckle at that and his tension drains a little bit.

"The real question is this Mason." I kneel up closer and instead of him moving away he freezes. "Do you find me attractive?"

He sighs, "Of course I do Ice, you're fucking gorgeous."

"Good, I feel the same about you. I want you. I'm not asking for more than this. If it's not something you like or are comfortable with, we can do it just this once and never even mention it again. I'll tell everyone some man named Yin took my virginity in a bar stall."

His fists are balled against his leg, but he's still not moving. I can see the hesitation all over his face. He thinks it's wrong, but I know it's right.

"Isley, I ..." He's going to try and talk himself out of doing this, but I don't want to give him the chance.

I push up from the floor and lightly swipe my lips across his. His eyes are wide open and I pull back only slightly. We are breathing each other's breath and our noses are still touching.

"Mason, I need you." I put all my emotions into the words and will myself not to cry, but I can feel my chest getting tight. A second feels like an hour as he stares at me. Just as I'm about to get up and run out the room, Mason's hand whips out. He cups the side of my neck, his large hand curling up to the base of my skull as he claims my mouth in a savage kiss. My fantasies didn't hold a candle to the real thing.

CHAPTER

10

YANG

No, fuck no. I can't do this. She's too young and inexperienced.

The little devil on my shoulder pipes in at that precise moment, "Yeah, completely inexperienced. Break her in Yang. You always knew that pussy was made for you."

No! No! No! She doesn't deserve just some quick romp. She deserves someone who can love her more than any man has ever loved a woman. Except I can't do that for her. She's too good for someone like me.

"Isley, I ..." Every single thought I had in my head disappears as her pillow soft lips brush against mine. The kiss was short and feather light. It was sensual and confident. It was all my will power could take.

"Mason, I need you." The words echo in my head. Words I had always been ashamed to hear in my personal fantasies of her. I'd imagine from time to time what it would be like to hear her say something like this, but I didn't expect it to be so fucking hypnotizing. In my head I would say some cool shit, but I didn't have the mental capacity now that she had actually said it in real life. My caveman instincts kick in instantly rendering me speechless and only able to act. I have to give her what she needs. Nothing else is more important than that right now. I grab the back of her neck and possessively claim her lips. She lets out a surprised moan and I swallow that helpless cry down. The sound only adding more fuel to my own needs. My cock is rock hard and I'm already about to come. Though I have barely touched her.

I stand up and bring her with me. I have to bend slightly, because she is that much shorter than I am. She moans into my mouth as our kisses build in intensity. She grabs hold of my kutte and closes the distance between our bodies. My sensitive cock presses into her stomach and her hips sway from side to side to get some friction of her own. She puts her hands under my shirt and that first contact of her trembling hands on my skin draws me back.

"Isley, are you fucking sure?" The question comes out hard and gruff. I don't let go of her neck I want to see any flicker of doubt in her eyes.

"I'm sure. Yes Mason. Yes." She raises back up on her tippy toes and this time she's attacking my mouth.

I run my hand along her back and find the zipper for her dress. I pull it down and she shimmies out of the dress. I nearly drop to my knees and thank God when I see what she has on underneath.

She is wearing a blood red bra and panties. They are a lacey material, that squeezes and pushes up her large tits. The panties are a high boy short that accentuates her hips. When she was younger Isley was always a very thin girl, but sometime between her junior year in high school and now she'd blossomed into this. I would compare her body to the typical picture of a burlesque dancer—Coca Cola bottle shape.

"This for me?" I step back to fully appreciate her and hopefully slow myself down a bit, or this shit was going to be over before it even started.

Her large bright blue eyes lock onto mine. Her lips part slightly and she reaches over her head and pulls the clip she was using to hold her hair up. Her long dark locks fall like a silk sheet down her back. She looks like a fucking angel.

"It's all for you Mason." She whispers before she pulls her chin up and shifts her weight to one side causing her ass to poke out a bit. I'll never forget this vision. No matter what happens in my life, when I die and my life flashes before my eyes this is going to be the last image I see.

"You're so fucking sexy." Enough appreciating, I grab hold of her again and return to mercilessly kissing her. I let my hands roam down her body. Stretching my fingers when I get down to her ass and squeeze both cheeks using them as a handle to press her into me.

We nip at each other and when she sucks my bottom lip into her mouth, I see fucking stars. Her hands go up to my kutte and she tries to push it off. I help her by shrugging out of it before I rip my face away from hers for a second and toss it on the loveseat behind us. I pull my shirt over my head in the same instant, an impressed sound bubbles out of her mouth as her hands roll over my abs. I'll never miss a workout with Archer again.

She examines me for only a second before she is kissing me again. She kisses my mouth and lets out a breathy moan as I graze my stubbly face along hers before I drop my mouth to her neck. That small tremble in her hands is gone. I want her to be as comfortable as possible. If she is choosing to give me this gift, I need to accept it properly.

I keep pushing her back until her knees hit the bed. She sits down and moves a pair of jeans I have hanging on the footboard before she reaches for my pants. I jump back so she can't touch. I'm already on edge if she touches me right now, I'll make a fool out of myself. A slight pout settles on her face, but I don't leave her waiting for too long. I race to kick out of my jeans and underwear, my boots come off along with them.

"All the way back." I order her and she lowers herself down to the bed. I pull her panties off, licking my lips in anticipation. Even her fucking pussy is pretty. I crawl onto the bed and she opens up for me thinking that I'm going straight into fucking her. I settle over her, my dick, rigid and leaking precum from the slit lays heavily on her stomach. I reach behind her and undo her bra. She shrugs it off and reaches her arms out to pull me down. I allow her to pull my top half down and I continue kissing on her swollen lips. I press urgent kisses down her jawline and suck on her neck. She hums in approval and her leg moves up and down on my side. I move lower and grab her tits with both my hands. When I enclose one pebbled nipple in my mouth her body jerks up and she moans loudly.

Her passionate sounds match her, deep and raspy. Still very feminine, with just a bit of grit. The moans along with her gasps and greedy pulling is driving me crazy. I trail my lips down the center of her stomach which causes her to shiver.

"You don't ..."

"You said it was all for me." I snap my eyes up to her. I didn't want to hold back, I feel like I've waited forever for this opportunity.

"All yours." She leans back and I push her legs open as far as they can go. Surprised to find that there was no tension, she straightens her knees and presents herself to me in a full split.

"Oh fuck." I take a mental picture of this and drop my forehead to her thigh. I was going to come. I press my hands to the back of her knees and hold her in this position, her pussy is fully open for me.

The first swipe of my tongue is all I need to know I'm addicted to eating Ice out.

"That's ... it's intense... so good." Her words are full of surprise. If she was a virgin maybe it meant no one had ever done this either. "No one sucked on this pretty pussy before?" I ask my mouth barely moving from where I want so desperately to be.

"No, never. Just you. Oh God, please do it again." She begs and tries to push herself down onto my mouth.

Knowing that this is her first time having someone suck her pussy makes me want to do a great job. I suck and flick my tongue over that sensitive nub. When she begins to writhe and pull away, I switch to her tight hole. I roll my tongue and fuck her with it before I slide back up and engulf as much of her as I can with my mouth. I flick the tip of my tongue quickly and her body coils up rushing towards release. Her legs are shaking and she tries to close them. I let her to an extent, because I have to use my hand to hold her down on the bed.

"Oh Mason, more, more, more." She begs and I comply. Her body jerks and a deep guttural groan comes out her mouth. On the first contraction her hands fly up into her hair. Her head whips back and forth as she fights to get away.

I haven't had enough of her yet. I keep her there, her dripping pussy against my face and I continue to push her past the point of breaking.

"I can't take it. Oh God. It's so good." She moans and cries. Her entire body is still shuddering and I feel her sit up. My eyes pop up to her, but my mouth stays sealed to her slit. Her long hair flows down one side of her body and she threads her fingers into my hair. She rolls her hips on my face and bites her lip as she watches me get her off.

That sight is more than I can take. I let go of her other leg and grab hold of my cock. I stroke myself hard desperate to release.

"No, don't finish. Please don't leave me like this." Her eyes glisten with tears that I know she will shed at any minute.

I lean my face back so she can hear me. "Don't worry, I just need to do this first one. I'm too excited. It'll be done too soon."

She nods her head and I go back to licking her pussy. She

lets her head fall back and moans my name. Three hard spurts pulse out of my dick and I have to turn my head to her inner thigh. I bite her there lightly and she hisses out in pain, but doesn't pull away.

Oh, my girl likes a little pain. Fuck yes.

My cock deflates only slightly, but one look at her and I know it won't stay like that for long. I only hope that small release is enough to take the edge off. I want to make this last for her. I want her to remember that her first lover wasn't a minute man.

When she comes on my mouth for the second time she falls back down to the bed and I crawl up her body. "Ice, I need you to look at me."

Her eyes find mine and lock on. "I'm going to try and be as gentle as I can. You need to tell me if you want me to stop at any time. You understand?"

"I don't want you to stop." She tries to pull me down on her and disregard what I'm saying.

"Isley, I'm serious. I don't want you to grit and bare it. If it hurts too much, tell me to stop."

"Ok, ok." She nods her head.

My entire body is aching to be inside of her. I drop my face down to hers and kiss her deeply, letting her taste her own juices on my lips. She licks it all up and has me wondering what she would do to my dick.

Next time.

I force the thought out of my head. There will be no next time. This is a one time thing. I've never been with a virgin before. I only know what my friends have told me and what

I've seen in movies. I didn't know how bad it could hurt her. I didn't want to hurt her. I rub the head of my cock up and down her slick opening before I press the large tip where it's supposed to be. I push in, but even though she is extremely wet I don't move forward.

"I think you have to go harder." She whispers as she trails her hand up and down my tricep.

"Fuck, ok." I press in even harder and it feels like I'm pressing against a warm sheet of muscle. Almost like there is no further opening there. I feel a different sensation right at the very tip. I can feel the edges of the hole I'm supposed to ram through, it didn't seem any bigger than a fucking dime. There was no way I would get in there without hurting her. "Isley, you're too tight. I'm too big for this."

"No, please. Let's try. Please?" One tear falls from her eye and I quickly wipe it away.

I place a hand on her hip and make sure to keep eye contact with her as I literally force the head of my dick inside of her. The thin tissue that is holding me out stretches, but the ring is still so tight around me I know she hasn't torn yet.

"Keep going." Her face is tight in pain and I push harder. When nothing happens, I grunt and push again. This time I get to the top of my shaft and I feel a sharp release. She gasps loudly and her hands clench the sheet underneath her.

"Isley. Fuck." I need to know if she's ok, but something deep inside overrides that. My need to get deeper inside of her takes over. I'd heard stories about people losing control and fucking so hard, they end up in the hospital. I never understood how that could be possible. I get it now. I would fuck Isley until my heart stopped beating if it meant I could feel more of this. She was so fucking tight. It's like every ridge in her pussy is tied tight around my cock. I push further in and her hand slaps against my side.

"Wait. Don't move." She whimpers and more tears fall.

The nerves in my body are shooting a million signals a minute. Half of me is urging me to push forward and the other half of me is telling me to stop. I battle internally while I wait for her to say anything else. She raises her hand and caresses my face. I focus on that and the trust on her face.

"Ok, slow. I need to get used to you." Her voice soothes all the chaos inside and just like before I comply with her wishes. I push into her torturously slow. When I get about three quarters of the way in, she stops me again.

"Mason, I don't think anymore will fit. Is this ok. Can we do it like this?"

I want to be deeper, but she knew her body better than me. I want to rectify that. I want to know every inch of her. "What are you feeling? Tell me what's going on inside."

I pull back and pump into her slowly making sure to stop pushing in before I went too far.

"I feel so stretched, you're everywhere. I feel you everywhere Mason." She licks her lips and closes her eyes as she starts to get used to what I'm making her feel. I stay at the slow pace until she grabs my hand and places it on her chest.

"You want more?" I am having a hard time keeping myself in check. I don't ever want to hurt her, but she's killing me right now.

"I don't know if I can." Her back arches up as I tweak her nipples between my fingertips.

"I'm going to try ok."

"Mmhmm."

I push in a little more and she moans, but doesn't tell me to stop. I go even faster, but still don't sink all the way into her.

"Oh, fuck that feels good. Can you make me come like this? Oh mmmm." Her hands go back into her hair. I watch her scratch at her scalp lightly and tug on her hair. I don't know if she realizes she's doing it, but I do. When she wraps her legs around my waist and helps me thrust, I know that she is all the way with me.

"You got what you want Isley? This good enough for you." I lean down and kiss at her mouth and face. She whimpers and really starts grinding down on my cock.

"It's perfect." She answers me.

I curl my arms under her shoulders until my hands are in her hair on either side of her head. I get a good grip, "Not yet." I tighten my grip on her hard at the same time as I thrust myself all the way inside of her. She lets out a loud gasp and her mouth falls into a perfect O. I tug her head back and her eyes roll in her head.

"God, yes Mason. Fuck me."

She's my own personal siren, I have no choice but to obey. I pump into her hard and fast. Part of me worries that I might be hurting her, but she rolls her hips. With every thrust she breaths fast and her eyes lock onto mine almost in surprise as her body careens into another orgasm. "I'm coming. Oh ...

yes." There was very little build up, but the strength of it has me moaning out my own pleasure. I fuck her through the rolling contractions deep inside of her. I was too far gone now. I let go of her hair and grip her hip to bang into her. She cries out and drags her nails down my back. I rear up from the sudden pain, but that only makes me thrust harder. Her legs lay over my thighs hooked around my hips and she turns her upper body to the side. "Mason, if you make me come again. I'll never fucking talk to you again." She moans and her back arches. I throw my head back and laugh, but never stop pumping into her. It was like a fucking challenge. Now I needed to do it. Her hands grab the sheets and she holds on while I take her on a ride. I want to see more of her. I take one of her legs and swing it to the side so her whole body is laying sideways. It's a different position and a new feeling for her. Her small waist is the perfect handle as I pull her back and forth on my dick. Her plump ass juts out as I thrust into her.

Her groans and whimpers grow louder and rougher as we continue. I watch her ass jiggle from the side and know if this is the last time I'm going to have her, I want to see what her ass looks like from the back.

"On your fucking knees." I bend over and growl into her ear.

She doesn't hesitate, she's a little wobbly, but she manages to pull her knees up and get into the position that I asked.

Her legs are on either side of me. I push her back down and grab the very tips of her hair to roll the strands around my hand. I tug slightly so her head is off the bed.

Every artist has their best piece of art, for Leonardo Di Vinci it's the Mona Lisa. For Isley, it's her ass. I could stare at her ass all fucking day and never get tired of it. I pump into her once and the ripple from my pelvis through her ass has me wanting to bend down and kiss her. This is the final position, I won't be able to last.

"I'm going to fuck you so hard right now. You're so damn sexy." I slap her ass lightly once and she groans, wiggling her ass against me. "Fuck." I wrap her hair around my fist one more time getting an even deeper arch in her back. I grab hold of her hips and let my body do what it's been wanting to do since we started. Fuck.

I've never been a very vocal person while I had sex. A grunt here or there and one when I come, but I can't stop the moans that are coming out of my mouth. I've never felt pussy like this. I doubt I ever will again. This is the best nut I've ever had in my life and I haven't even had it yet.

"Mason, you're so deep. I'm close. Don't stop. Fuck don't stop."

I don't have a choice so I do what I can to speed her along. I tug harder on her hair knowing that she really likes it. I adjust myself so I hit a different angle and at the first thrust Isley nearly runs off my cock. I grab hold of her waist and continue.

"Oh dammit!" She grips the wrist of the hand that I have at her waist. She digs her nails in as she grabs the pillow in front of her with the other hand and slams it to her mouth. She screams loud into the pillow and her entire body clenches hard on my dick.

"That's it, Ice. Fuck yes." I let go of her hair to grab handfuls of ass. I slam into her with a loud groan, my orgasm feels like it's never going to be over. I collapse on top of her and wish for the sweet release to end, but even after my cock is no longer shooting out cum my body feels like it's in a state of hypersensitivity. The warmth of her pussy, the sound of her soft whimpers, the thunderous beating of my heart—the absolute best orgasm I have ever had in my life.

"I can't breathe." She mutters out and I quickly move to the side. I don't slide out of her, but just transfer my weight onto the bed. I grab her by the waist and turn her with me. I curl around her and fall asleep with the best girl I've ever been with in my arms. She's like my own personal fucking angel and I don't want to let her go.

CHAPTER 11

YANG

My head feels as if it's going to pop off my body at any second. The sound of my blood pulsing through my veins is enough to make me cringe in pain. I don't remember the last time I had a hangover like this. I don't want to open my eyes in case there is any light. My stomach is rolling and it feels like a cat shit on my tongue. I should know better than to drink that damn much. Fuck.

I lift one arm, but there is something heavy and warm on the other one.

"Who the fuck?" My voice sounds like a croaking frog. I slit open one eye. Thankfully either it's still night or none of the lights are on. Long dark hair covers the face of a woman sleeping next to me. A soft snore leaves her mouth and dark pouty lips peek out through the layers of hair.

I do my best to think back on what had happened last night, but everything is still fuzzy. I must have really been out of it if I let one of the club bunnies sleep in my room. I've never done no shit like that. I pull my arm from under the woman's head and her hair falls away from her face as she rolls over to her back.

"No! No! What the fuck! No!" Panic erupts in my pounding head as I look down at Isley in all her naked glory. She doesn't even have a cover on. I would never fuck her. Did I? This is fucking bad. Fuck! I sit up in the bed and can feel my midsection and thighs are sticky. There is dried cum everywhere and also blood. There is quite a bit on me, but I can see more on her thighs. Not only did I fuck her, but I took her virginity.

I'm going straight to fucking hell. This was the last straw. I drag a hand down my face and calm myself enough to try to remember what happened. The night came back in flashes until all the flashes began to play like an HD movie.

I'd fucked her.

She'd wanted me to. She said I was the best option to get rid of her virginity. That it was a one time thing. I remember her moans and the way she cried when she thought I wouldn't have sex with her. I remember her rolling her hips as my cock sank in and out of her pussy. I remember the feel of her tight cunt giving way as I plunged into her for the first time. Yeah, no amount of alcohol would ever get me to forget that.

It was the best fucking night of my life, but now I'm going to have to pay the consequences. My sister is going to fucking kill me. It shouldn't have been me who took her virginity. What if she was drunk and now, she regrets that this shit happened? I couldn't give it back. What if I had hurt her, there was a lot of blood. What if …

"Oh fuck. Oh no. Fuck." I jump off the bed and move the sheets around. I check the garbage can and then I look down at my dick. It's still sticky and coated with our juices and her blood.

"Mason?"

My eyes pop up to her. I hadn't even realized she woke up.

"Isley." My voice is hard and I say her name with disgust.

I watch as she instantly puts her guard up. "What the hell is your problem?"

"My problem, all of this is my fucking problem right now!" I yell at her, I'm fuming mad and I have no one to take it out on, but her. "Do you remember what happened last night?"

"What? Yes, I remember what happened last night. I told you I wasn't drunk."

"I wish I could say the fucking same." I shake my head and walk to the middle of my room, "We shouldn't have fucking done this. God dammit. What the fuck were you thinking!" I go back to blaming her.

She jumps out of bed and glares at me. "Me? You seemed pretty into it last night. You telling me you don't remember anything we did last night?"

"I remember it, doesn't mean I was thinking straight when we did it. For fuck's sake did we even use a condom?" I throw my hands up in frustration.

Her eyes drop down to my limp cock and her eyes widen slightly. "Fuck, no. We didn't. Fuck." She falls back down on the bed and tugs her hands through her hair. A flashback of me wrapping her long locks around my hand replays in my head. Fuck I want to do it again.

"Are you clean?" She asks me, her voice low.

"Maybe that's something you should have asked before you begged me to fuck you."

She stares at me, her eyes watering up and her chin trembling.

"Look, yeah I'm clean, but that's not the only thing that you need to worry about with unprotected sex. I'm sure your parents told you about the stork. Spoiler, the baby doesn't fall from the sky it pops out your pussy."

"Mason, I'm on the shot so I don't have to worry about that." She stands up from the bed again and walks closer to me. "I understand that this is a bit of a shock to you, but everything is fine now. You're overreacting." She raises her hand to touch me and I back away like she's an open flame.

"Yeah, you're right. Everything is good. We never have to talk about this shit again. I can pretend like it never happened."

"Pretend it never happened? I thought ... I mean I thought it was good."

Good it was fucking mind blowing and it will never be topped, "Ice, I'm never fucking touching you again. I can barely fucking look at you right now. This was a bad idea. I regret ever fucking touching you."

She gasps and reels back like I'd just slapped her in the face. "You fucking asshole."

"Fuck this." I toss a hand up and walk over to the bathroom, I slam the door and turn the water on. I quickly wipe myself off and towel dry before I look up into the mirror. I'm panicked. I don't remember the last time I was ever this rattled. I take a few breaths and ask myself why. I may play it up that I was drunk and I was, but I knew what I was doing. I'd wanted her. Fuck I still want her. It was a beautiful thing that we did last night and I had to ruin it this morning by acting like a piece of shit. She'd trusted me. Even though I knew that I still made this a bad experience for her, I'm not mad at her. She knew what she wanted and she went for it. I'm mad that I allowed myself to sully something as pure as she is. I don't deserve her. She should have the white picket fence, a dog and children. She shouldn't be running around behind a degenerate biker. I'm not for her and I hate myself for forgetting that in such a spectacular way. I hear a door slam.

What the fuck? "Ice?" I call out. I open my bathroom door and she's gone. "Fuck wait!" I call for her. I run out the bathroom, but I'm still naked. I grab the first pair of basketball shorts I see hanging around and burst out my room.

Everyone is already outside sitting in the main area having breakfast when I come flying out. Isley doesn't say a word as she storms out of the club and no one stops her. I chase after her, but by the time I get to the door she is already in her car. Huge cracks of lightning stop me in my tracks. I stand right there in the doorway of the club as torrential rain pours down and thunder rolls through the sky. She glances in my direction and I expect to see anger, pure rage in her eyes instead I see sadness and disappointment. I'd done that. She drives off, leaving me there with tension and my own anger trying to push its way through my pores. I had her and lost her all in one fucking night.

CHAPTER

YANG

I turn back into the clubhouse; my entire chest feels like it's being crushed under a mysterious weight. I've never felt like more of an asshole in my life. I shouldn't have run her out of here like that. My muscles feel like they are quivering as I think about how hurt she'd looked. If anyone else had put that fucking look on her face it would be cause for me to fuck them up, but this time it was me.

It's for the best.

I know I can't let her think that we have a way of being together. I'm not made for her. I can't allow her to get her hopes up. I want her too though. The pain in my chest doubles as my anger intensifies, I want her to still be in my bed. I want to wake up next to her the same way I had this morning. My fucking soul is being torn in two and I'm here trying to convince myself that it'll be ok to live this way. It won't, I don't think anything will ever be the same after last night.

"Yang, do we need to go get her?" Bones is the first one to speak up. At least the first one that I hear. I shake my head no and walk over to my room. I need to get myself under control. Worse things have happened. At least I was able to share in that moment with her.

I walk into my room and the emptiness of it suddenly strikes me as abnormal. It's off. The place I'd once found my peace, now fucking feels like a strange place. Is it the loveseat? Is it, because the sheets are rumpled? Is it, because there's no lights? What the fuck is it?

I grab for the sheets on my bed and pull them back. I just need to get the place cleaned up and I'll feel better.

The second I see the blood smears on the bed it's like my brain completely checks out. All the emotions I've been trying to stuff down come rushing to the top like an unopened, shaken soda can.

"Fuck! Motherfucking asshole!" I grab the frame of my entire bed and flip it to the side of the room. It flies across the room, but that doesn't make me feel any better. I grab for the garbage can and sling it against the wall. I pick my feet up and put a hole through the small end table causing the lamp to fly off and crash on the floor. "You piece of shit!" I roar. When I find there is nothing else I can get to, I turn my anger on the wall. I punch it like it's my enemy. I punch the wall like I'm punching myself in the face. I hear myself scream out again. There are no more words now it's just rage leaving my mouth.

"Yang! Fucking hell." Someone grabs me, but I shake them off without looking back. Blood starts to pour from my knuckles, but it's not enough. I deserve so much fucking worse than this. More arms try to close around me. It's too much. I feel like I'm fucking suffocating. I shake them off again. I'm being attacked. I turn and fall into my defensive stance. I can't even see the faces of the people around me. Everything is clouded in fog. What the fuck is going on?

Someone steps in from my right and I raise my hands ready to swing. Another person in front of me takes a step and I swing. I don't hit anything, but the person to the right flicks his hand and the contact is so severe that it literally knocks some sense into me. I stumble back and shake my head.

"Yang!" Someone calls my name. While I'm focused on the person to my right, someone grabs me by my face and turns my head. "Brother, come back. Come on."

Archer is sweating and his eyes are boring into mine. My heart stutters and I fucking want to cry. Why does this shit feel so fucking intense? I blink a few times and focus on my president. I concentrate and realize that the people around me are my club. Jameson's shirt is ripped, Bones has a bloody lip, and Lex is standing against the wall with his hands up.

"Yang!"

Fuck I had attacked them. Fuck. I drop right there and Archer follows me down. "I'm sorry. I'm so fucking sorry." I have to swallow the frog in my throat.

"What the fuck happened? Who was that girl?"

"Ice." It even hurts to say her name.

"Ice, holy shit! Isley!" I hear Tink somewhere.

Archer turns his head I'm assuming to where she is. I keep my eyes locked on the ground trying to get my body back into its natural state. I don't remember the last time I've raged out like this. It had to be back when I was in the military.

"Who's Isley?"

"Uh, I think she's his little sister's best friend."

"Yikes." Shyne says.

"You can say that shit again." It's the first normal thing to come out of my mouth.

"Isn't that the same girl from last night, the one you said you weren't going to fuck?" Jameson tilts his head. I can't deal with his judgement right now.

"Wait a minute, you said little sister's best friend. Tell me that girl was of age." Archer demands going over what Jameson had asked.

"Yeah, barely, she's nineteen."

"Fucking cradle robber." Shyne snarks out. It's a joke. I know it's a joke except I see nothing but red. I lunge for him and Jameson has to step in the way so I don't grab him.

"Shut your fucking mouth! Fuck you Shyne!"

He didn't realize that I would get this upset so quickly. "My bad, I was playing. Fuck, cool out." He puts his hands up. "Shit, I've never seen you like this. You're losing your shit." His eyes are wide, he's telling the truth. I'm flying way the hell off the handle.

I grit my teeth and sharp pain shoots through my jaw.

"Settle the fuck down Yang!" Archer screams in my face, "That's a fucking order!"

I fall back down to the ground sitting against the wall.

"I shouldn't have. She didn't ..." I don't finish my thought.

"You better not be saying that you forced yourself on that woman?" Jameson snarls at me.

"What, no. I didn't rape her. She wanted it. She came here for it."

"What does that mean?" Bones questions.

"According to her I was the best decision. She said she was tired of waiting on some man to not be a jerk. So, because she's known me for so long and knows my character, I was the best choice to be her first."

"Wait, you took her fucking virginity?" Tink squeals out. I still don't know where she is, maybe right outside the door.

"You will keep your mouth shut. I shouldn't even be talking about this shit."

"Hell, brother. I don't understand why you're so torn up then. If you know for sure that she wanted this, that she came here solely looking for this, what is the problem? You did what she asked." Jameson shrugs his shoulder.

"I agree, this doesn't sound like a problem." Archer says from where he is sitting in front of me.

"It is. It's a problem, because Ice isn't one of the girls that you just fuck and toss away. She needs some Fortune 500 dude, someone who could build her a white picket fence. Fucking carriage rides and shit. I don't have none of that inside of me. She deserves fucking better than what I gave her, I'm just another fucking jerk and I feel like I took advantage of her. Hell, you saw her running out this morning. It only took me a minute from the time I woke up with this killer ass hangover to get her to start crying. I don't want to hurt her, but that's all I know how to do."

Archer nods his head, contemplating exactly what he wanted to say to me. "Is it better for her that you let it go? Are you sure there is someone else that can treat her better?"

"Without a doubt. I shouldn't have fucked her."

"Then let her be. She'll be mad for a while, but she'll get over it. You can't let it tear you up like this. You're no good to anyone the way you are right now." Archer pounds softly on the top of my shoulder with his fist.

"Yeah, I know. My bad again guys. I lost it. I'm with it now." I wasn't really, but I was as close as I was going to get.

"That's what we are here for." Jameson puts his hand down and helps me up. Archer gets up as well.

"Before I clean this shit up, who hit me?" I look around the room.

"I did, you were swinging at Archer." Lex speaks up. He was up front about it, but I could see the anxiety in his face. He had hit a patched member. As a prospect, no matter the case, hitting a patched member should be instant disqualification.

"Do we need to vote on this?" Archer asks. It's my right to say I want Lex out.

"No way, but I will say this." I turn to Lex, "Bro, I'm never fighting you fair. Ever. You hit like a fucking sledgehammer. What the fuck." I rub my jaw and he laughs.

"You should have felt my punch before they shoved nails through my hands."

"Fuck that, I would have been a fucking dead man." I wasn't even exaggerating. Even in my rage fueled mania that punch had me questioning my decisions in life. "Thanks for that. I wouldn't have forgiven myself if I'd hit him. But now you get to help me clean this shit up."

Lex jumps right to action and the rest of the guys turn to file out, but Pirate is walking in.

"We good." I tell him thinking that he is coming to see if he can help me.

"Nah, we not good. We got a problem." Pirate looks over to Archer.

"What is it?"

"Clay is freaking the fuck out, he is actually over there crying. He has some information, but he says he feels like you're going to kick him out. He's going on and on about how we are his only family and how he didn't mean to forget."

"God damn it." Archer pushes through and the rest of us follow him.

I turn and call over my shoulder, "Lex, just leave the bed. Pick up what you can, I'll clean it later." I hustle to catch up with the rest of the club members. My previous emotional breakdown gone and now my focus is on what kind of problem could be going on to shake Clay. He's a fucking good prospect and he knows that we all really care for him. So, for him to think that we would kick him out it must be something really bad. When we all walk out to the main space and I see his face, I know it's as bad as I was thinking.

CHAPTER

13

YANG

"I'm fucking sorry. I was trying to make sure everything was right yesterday. I forgot ... it didn't even seem wrong last night, but I forgot." Clay is visibly upset. He's not crying now, but I can see the red around his eyes. Evidence that he was.

"What are you talking about? You're talking fucking gibberish right now." Archer chides.

"I swear I didn't do this shit on purpose." Clay went on, but still didn't say shit about what he was talking about.

"Hey, calm the fuck down and just tell us what happened." I raise my voice, but I do my best not to be too forceful. "Take a breath."

He does and I watch as his shoulders relax a little bit. Finally, after a second or two he starts to talk. "Last night right when we were in the thick of things someone came up to the door. I thought it was another party goer, but they didn't come in. Instead, they just gave me a folded piece of paper and told me to give it to Archer when I had a chance. They didn't act like it was urgent. When I took it and turned to the person next to me to check them, they wandered off. I didn't think about it again until this morning when I pulled it out of my pocket and started to read it."

"Give it here." Archer puts his hand out and Clay reaches into his back pocket. He pulls out a single sheet of folded paper and hands it over to Archer.

His eyes go wide and he pulls the sheet closer to his face as if he can't believe what he is reading.

"Motherfucker! Fuck!" Now Archer is the one who is losing his shit, "Pirate get the fuck on the phone and find out what the count was last night. Get that room secured now. Jameson, Shyne, fuck … everyone else I need all the workers from the Casino accounted for, right the fuck now."

A buzz of panic filters through the air.

"What's going on?" Jameson asks.

"Move! Now!" Archer screams out before he runs towards the church.

Pirate walks by me and over to Clay. He grabs the prospect by his rags and shakes him. "What the fuck was on that paper?"

"I don't know all of it."

"Say what you know!" Pirate screams.

"I saw what looks like security codes, addresses, and names. I saw the name Bull."

Fuck. It was starting. We were fucking under attack.

Jameson, Shyne, Pirate, and I jump in the truck and high tailed it to the casino. It was pouring, so taking our bikes was out of the question. Everything appears to be normal when we get there. No one's running, screaming, or bleeding to death on the floor.

Pirate heads straight to the counting room while the rest of us run towards the main security station. Herb, our floor manager is in there with a cup of coffee. He jumps out his seat and spills some on his shirt when we burst through the door.

"Herb, I need a list of all the employees that are supposed to be at work today and I need to know if they've checked in. I need that shit yesterday." Jameson quickly barks out. Usually that would be a strange request, but Herb is used to doing strange things for us.

"Working on it." He turns to the computer and starts to compile the list that we ask him for.

"I'm going to walk around the perimeter and see if there is anything out of the ordinary." I tell him, he nods his head and I take off. "Shyne, you got my back?"

"Right behind you brother."

The actual casino is on a large piece of land that is just a few blocks from the main town. If there was something catastrophic to happen here like a bomb or some shit more people would get hurt.

"What are we looking for?" Shyne asks as I slowly walk and scan everything.

"Anything that seems out of the ordinary, hell even shit that looks like it should be there, but wasn't before. Anything new. Anything broken down." I tell him and he busies himself looking in the opposite direction as I am.

"You know I didn't mean nothing by that, what I said earlier, right?"

"Bro not right now. I need to focus."

"Got it" He replies.

We scan the entire outside. It takes us hours, but we have to be sure that nothing is there that would be a security breach. When we get back, we are soaked. Jameson and Pirate have gone through most of the list of employees. So far everything is checking out as on point.

"You think that bastard would actually be dumb enough to come after the people that we work with?" Shyne asks.

"I don't know," Pirate says, "what I'm concerned about is how the fuck did he know those codes? Only our people know them. He had all of them spot on. What the fuck else does he know?"

"Anyone see anything crazy or have anyone come up to them?" I ask Jameson about the employees.

"No, no one knows anything." He cracks his knuckles as we look for the last person on the list. Once we go through everyone to ensure that this was just a scare and no one is actually in any danger we make our way back to the clubhouse.

"Yeah, you fucked up! You can't be a part of this club if we can't trust you to do your fucking job. Clay, I don't know what I'm going to do with you, but right now I want you to get the hell out of my face."

When we walk in Archer is screaming on Clay. Daria is standing to the side waiting on Archer to come back to her. She must be planning to calm him down. We went from having a good time last night to possibly being in the middle of an attack.

"What did you find out?" Archer asks when he notices us.

"No one is hurt. All of the information was correct though. Pirate had to change all the codes to the vault and cash boxes, but nothing else out of the ordinary. The workers say they haven't seen anything strange.

"Yeah, they don't need to know something is going down for something to be going down. This is fucking ridiculous." Archer pinches the bridge of his nose as he takes in a few breaths. "The letter was from Bull; he says we need to talk again about them protecting us. Why the fuck are we the ones who need protecting? How the fuck were they able to infiltrate us so easily? I need some fucking answers here, because last I fucking checked we aren't some third-rate motorcycle club. This shit isn't something that should be happening to us. Someone needs to find out how the fuck it did and now." He roars out. "I don't know what needs to be done, but I know I want everyone focused," Archer levels his stare at me, "on the job at hand. Next time they come looking for information I want to catch them in fucking action."

We all nod, this wasn't a discussion, this was an order.

At the moment I felt bad for Clay, he might have been overwhelmed at the time, but that shouldn't have stopped him from getting that paper to Archer last night. If something crazy had gone down while he was sitting on that information, him being screamed on would have been the last thing he would need to worry about.

There's a lot of backend work that needs to be done if we

are going to find out how Bull and his Drift Demons were able to get into our system. We needed to get started on it right away.

Even with everything that is going on my mind tries to drift over to thoughts of Isley, but I don't have time for that. I'm the one that's supposed to be keeping everyone on task. I have to make sure that I do too.

CHAPTER 14

YANG

After hours of combing through security footage and emails, we were no closer to finding out how Bull had got the information. Archer refuses to even sit down and talk with the man. This wasn't someone who was trying to help us. Bull was trying to do exactly what his name implies, barge into our little world and take it over. Archer might be a quiet man, but he's not a pushover. None of us are.

Once the initial shock of everything is starting to wear off my mind goes back to Ice. I do everything I can to stop it but, I can't stop. It's like my own personal form of punishment. I get a taste of something that I've wanted for years only to realize that it's better than I have ever imagined and I will never have it again.

My hangover has finally gone away and I'm ravenous.

I pull out something from the fridge to eat. Only all I can think about is if she has a hangover today? She's so fucking young. I shouldn't have let her drink no matter what she said to me. Maybe I should call Christina just to make sure that

Isley got home ok. It was pouring when she peeled out of here this morning.

I didn't even realize that someone else had walked into the kitchen with me.

"You going to get something out or are you just checking the temperature?" Celine jokes with me and I jump in surprise.

"Shit, sorry." I close the fridge and step away ready to go back to the back room where Jameson and Bones were looking though some more video footage.

"You were thinking about that girl?"

I guess everyone knows about Ice. "Yeah. I'm distracted."

"Yeah, I can tell. I heard what you said about not being the right one for her." She leans against the table and crosses her arms over her chest.

"How did you hear that?" She wasn't there this morning. Ugh, fucking Tink. "Never mind."

"Don't be mad, we all just want to help."

"I don't need help I need someone to erase my memory. I need last night to not have happened at all." I admit.

"Are you sure? Is that what she would want too? If you want my opinion, I think you're being too hard on yourself."

She didn't understand, none of them did. "I'm not, trust me."

"Fine if you say so, but I'll say this. She chose you, and from what it seems like this must have been a long time in the making. It's not like you were the one pursuing her. She actively chose you, young or not, she's old enough to know what she wants. You have to let her make her own decisions."

"It's the wrong one." I bite out.

"To whom? The people who might judge you, because you are a little older than her? Those who still haven't got their shot at her? Who decides that it's the wrong one? How do you know she wants a white picket fence? Maybe she wants a red motorcycle instead."

The actual visual of her straddling a candy red bike burns itself in my mind. Even though I'm completely drained from all the fucking that we did last night, my cock jerks at the thought.

I don't reply to her, she's wrong. She has to be, but a small kernel of possibility starts to nestle in my mind. What if she does want the same things that I want? Can I be enough for her?

"Look, if you want this all to go away then do like Archer says. You're going to have to give her a lot of space. But if you are this torn up about it then maybe you need to listen to what your body and your mind is telling you and get that woman." She opens the fridge pulls out a water and walks out the kitchen squeezing my shoulder on her way out.

I didn't want to let myself think that being with Ice was a possibility. I didn't want to picture the way she'd moaned out my name as I made her come over and over again on my lips. I didn't want that, but as I've recently come to find out, I don't always get what I want.

By that night, everything had quieted down. Archer had decided to let Clay stay, but he was on very thin ice. One more thing goes wrong and he was out. I would do my best to make sure the kid stayed on the right track. I'd hate to lose a prospect like him.

We still weren't on lockdown, so a few people were still coming in and out of the clubhouse. Twig walks in with a small bag in her hand. She looks even better when she didn't have her stripper outfits on. If I saw her on the street, I would have definitely talked to her. She smiles in my direction before she turns and knocks on the door to Archer and Daria's room. Daria comes out and takes the bag from her. They talk for a little while, but I'm not interested enough to figure out what about. I told myself I needed to distract myself. Bones and Shyne were in the middle of a game of pool. I could have joined them, but I just didn't have the energy. Sitting there and listening to the bullshit that they were spewing to each other would have to be enough to distract me right now. I pick up the bottle of water that I have on the floor and take a swig. I'm still trying to get my fluids back to normal after all that alcohol I'd drunk last night. I don't need to ever drink like that again.

I hear Daria say thanks and then Twig makes her way over to where we all are.

"Hey boys."

She's a regular for us. Most of the club has some sort of relationship with her. She's a nice enough woman, never too much drama with her.

"What's up Twig? Everything good?" Bones asks her.

"Yeah, just needed to drop off something to Daria. Thought I would check on this one. He looks like he just lost his puppy." She gestures to me with her chin.

Shyne laughs, "Well he lost something." he says under his breath.

This motherfucker was asking for me to beat his ass. He watches me from the corner of his eye to see if I would get up and do just that, but I didn't move.

"Aww, I'm sorry. I was just playing around I didn't really want to you to be having a shitty day. " Twig sits down next to me on the couch.

"Yeah well, shit happens right."

She squints at me and then shakes her head. "That doesn't sound like you. I'm not sure If I like sad Yang." She pulls a small mirror thing from her purse and starts to fiddle with her lip gloss. "Is there anything that I could do to make you feel better? You know I'm always here if you want to talk."

I turn in her direction and focus on her face. She's still looking into the mirror. Did she really think that I was so desperate up that I would reach out to a fucking club bunny for someone to talk to? I'd rather go pay a fucking shrink first before I did that shit. The second that thought enters my mind I feel like an asshole. Just because the woman dances and fucks for money doesn't mean she's not a person. Here she was trying to be nice to me and I was putting her down, because of her profession. Technically I killed people for a living and people still sought me out to talk. "Yeah, I appreciate that. I think I'm going to be ok though."

"Yeah, you will." Bones says as he lines up his next shot. I ignore him. I was impressed that they all had so much faith in me.

"Come on, how about a little smile? I don't think I should leave here without seeing you smile just once." She finally puts the mirror away and turns in my direction.

"I guess you're going to be here for a while then. I don't really feel like smiling today."

"One good one and I'm out of your hair." Why can't I be like Bones or Jameson, all they have to do is fucking grunt at people and they run in the other direction. I'm the fucking nice one. "Twig, seriously just let it go."

She draws her leg up on the seat and leans over getting into my space. She lays feather kisses on my neck, but instead of it turning me on it just fucking tickles. Even though it's so fucking anti big scary biker dude, I'm ticklish as fuck.

I chuckle lightly before I draw my shoulder up to my cheek to get her to stop what's she's doing.

"Bro ..." Both Bones and Shyne stop what they are doing to look at me, "Did you just fucking giggle." Shyne stares at me with shock and barely contained excitement all over his face. This is one of those secrets you never really want your buddies to know about you.

"No, fuck you."

"The fuck you didn't. Twig do it again." Bones says and she obeys. She finds a space by my ear and does the same quick fluttery kisses there. I chuckle again and try to push her away. She wraps her arms around my neck and uses her fingers to tickle the other side of my neck. I can't hold back the loud laughter that comes out of my mouth as I move again to get her off.

"Holy shit! Someone get the fucking camera!" Shyne calls out.

"Twig get off of me. I'm not fucking with you." I do my best to sound menacing, but she pokes at my side. I clench up and laugh louder as she doubles down and really starts going at me. Bones is leaning heavily on the pool cue laughing his ass off while Shyne has his cell phone out I'm guessing to record my vulnerable moment.

A strong breeze blows across my face as the door to the club opens. I turn for a second to see who it is, but Lex quickly stands in front of the person. It's too late, I've already seen her and she's already seen me. Of course, Ice would pop back up right as there was another woman writhing away on my lap.

"Get the fuck off." I roar and toss Twig to the side. She squeals and lands on the couch. I don't bother to check on Twig. I get up and run to the door, pushing through Lex. For the second time today, I see Isley racing off in her car.

"Fuck man, I didn't see it was her until she took the hood of her jacket off." Lex says from next to me.

My heart hammers away in my chest as I stare at her tail-lights getting further and further away from me. I can't fucking believe this shit. How much worse could this get? How much more of an asshole could I make myself look?

I walk back in the clubhouse; my mind is in a complete fucking breakdown. I blink a few times before I start laughing. Complete fucking hysterics. This makes perfect fucking sense. Of course, she would show up right now.

"Well, fuck me." I hear Shyne say. "Archer, Yang's gonna blow up the clubhouse." He yells out.

Archer, Pirate, and Jameson come out of church.

Celine and Daria come out of her room.

"What the fuck is wrong with him?" Jameson asks.

I get myself under control, but the crazed hysterical laughing turns into uncontrollable rage. "Fuck! Fucking bitch!" I grab hold of the pool table and squeeze, the felt feels like sandpaper against my fingertips.

"Ah, that girl Ice came back." Lex says.

"Fuck" Pirate says.

"When Twig was humping him and kissing on his neck."

"Oh fuck!" Celine says.

I calm down. It's better this way. If she thought we would work this shit out or something at least now she'd know for sure that I'm no good for her. Twig just did me the biggest favor I could ask for. She'd put the nail in my coffin.

CHAPTER 15

ICE

"You dummy!" I slam my hand on the steering wheel, as I wait for the red light to change. I swipe the huge tears that are still falling from my eyes a full ten minutes after I drove away from the club. For the second time today, I've had to see Mason screaming out for me as I drove away. "You're so stupid." More tears fall.

Finally, the light changes and I pull into the parking lot of my off-campus dorm. I lock up my car and basically run to my room. I can't believe that I'm so stupid. I've spent years trying to get Mason to notice me. Forever trying to get him to see me as more than a little girl. I should have just let it go. How many times did he have to tell me that he didn't see me like that before I believed him? I went back, because I was sure that this morning was just a shock. He'd overreacted and was scared that I didn't know what I was doing. Whatever the problem was, I just knew that his reaction this morning wasn't really who he is. I'd gone back there, because I wanted him to admit that he could see how good we could be together. Based on the way that woman was all over his lap, it's clear that he's not as into me as I am into him.

I lay on the bed and just cry. Usually, I can get the water-works to shut off after a while, but my heart hurts so fucking much right now. I really trusted him. I know I'd told him that it could be a one time thing, but having him take me like he did last night did nothing to quell the desire I have for him. If anything, it only amplified it.

The front door opens and Christina walks in. "Ice, I have brownies and I'm not fucking sharing!" She drops whatever she has in the main room and walks over to my door with a brownie in her hand probably to taunt me with. The joking smile that she had on her face drops off when she sees the state that I'm in.

"Oh fuck! What's wrong, Isley? What happened? Are you ok?" She throws the treat on my nightstand and engulfs me in a big hug.

"I'm ... I'm ... Fi ... fin ..." I can't even get the words out before I wail even harder. I'm not fine and I don't want to lie to her. One of the worst parts about this whole ordeal is I'm too scared to even tell her what's really going on.

"Isley, I swear to God if you don't tell me right now what the fuck is going on, I'm going to lose my shit! Now fucking tell me." She grabs me by my arms and shakes me hard.

"I can't." I weep into her arms.

"Did it have something to do with last night? The boy you went on a date with?" She tries to catch my eyes, but I look away on purpose. "Fuck this I'm calling my brother. We're just going to kill everyone at that club." She spits out.

"No!" I scream at the top of my lungs and rip myself out of her arms. "Don't call him, ok? Just don't."

"I will if you don't tell me what the hell is going on. I'm fucking scared. What's wrong?"

I fold the hem of my shirt over and over; she's going to be pissed. I don't want to lose my best friend over this. She's honestly the only person in my life that I can count on no matter what. The summer my mother was locked up for DUI, she was the one who had hid me in her room and fed me until my mom was released. Even now, it's her money that pays for the lion's share of this apartment. I help out with my stipend, but most everything comes from her. I would be out on the street if it weren't for her.

If I tell her it was some random man, she'd call her brother. Then she'd demand to know who I was with and then tell him to fuck them up. If I tell her the truth, she may hate me forever for going after her brother. There are certain lines that you don't cross and I'd definitely crossed the line.

"Ice!" Christina calls out again.

"You're going to hate me. I'm scared to say it." I still don't have the guts to look at her.

"What? Why would I be mad at you? That's ridiculous. I love you like you're my sister, there is nothing that you could have done that would cause me to hate you." She smooths my hair down and rubs my back. "Just tell me."

"You know last night I went to that party so I could seduce the guy." I was just going to have to tell her and pray that she meant what she'd just said.

"Yeah, like we talked about. Did he hurt you, is that why you're crying?"

"No, well not exactly." I sigh and just spit it out. "There was no guy that I was bringing to meet me there, the guy was already there at the party. He lives there."

Christina's eyebrows cinched and she moves back. "He lives at the clubhouse?"

I nod, "I lost my virginity to your brother, Mason." I swallow and brace myself.

Her face goes slack and she stares at me, "What?"

I repeat what I said though I know she heard me. "The guy I've been talking about the past few days is Mason."

Her hands lift off my back and she moves away from me on the bed, turning her head to the other side so she doesn't have to look at me.

It starts. I should give her space, she's probably going to want me to move out. Fucking great.

I stand up and grab my bag.

"Where are you going?"

I turn back to Christina who looks confused. "I'm going away. You're upset, I totally get you need your space."

She rolls her eyes and lets out a deep sigh. "Dummy, sit down. I'm not mad at you."

I drop my purse down instantly. "You're not?"

"No, I turned away so you wouldn't see me gag. I still love you, but you for sure got the fucking cooties. That shit don't wash off either." She laughs and forms a cross with her two pointer fingers.

I laugh along with her before I start crying again. I sit back on the bed grateful that she was true to her word.

"See, I had long fantasies about how you would come home and tell me how you lost your virginity. And I would make you tell me every detail." She levels me with her intense brown eyes, "Ice please don't scare me like that. I want to know what's wrong, but I don't need to know how big, how little, how good, or how bad. I don't want any of those details please be as vague as humanly possible. For the love of God." She shudders and move close to me.

"Why are you not mad?" I shouldn't look a gift horse in the mouth, but I had to know.

"Please, I've known for years that you had a thing for my brother. I've seen your diary. I knew you loved him before, but I figured once you got older the phase would go away, except it never did. Then I figured once you got a boyfriend, you'd move on. But that never happened. You've been preparing me for this day since you first met him. I don't mind, we just can't share any sex stories, because I'll literally … die."

I pull her back in for a hug and she hugs me back. When I move back, I wipe my tears and get myself under control.

"Now the question is, how bad am I going to have to hurt my brother?" Her eyes squint in my direction and wait for me to continue with the story. I tell her everything, she was so excited that the plan had worked and then skeeves out when she realizes she had basically taught me how to get in her brother's pants. When it came to the actual sex part, I completely glossed over it just telling her that he could write a how to guide and he would be a billionaire overnight. She cringes, but smiled all the same. It wasn't until I got to what happened this morning that she got mad.

"It was completely bizarre, Christina, like he was disgusted to be with me. I know what I felt last night. It wasn't pity or only lust. He was taking care of me, he was trying to please me, he seemed like he wanted me." I sigh and continue, "I left after our argument came back here got changed and went to my classes. The more I thought about what happened the surer I became that it was all just shock. I mean I had been just his little sister's best friend only hours ago and now we were smack into something completely different. I went over there to talk to him, but I walked in the clubhouse to see another woman on his lap, kissing and humping on him."

"Eww! They were fucking right there out in the open?'

"I don't think they were fucking, but they were close. He was very comfortable with it and enjoying himself."

"That fucking bastard. I'll fuck him up. Don't worry." She pats my leg and takes out her phone. I put my hand on top of it before she can do anything.

"Please don't call him. Just let it go, ok? Soon it'll be a distant memory."

She smiles at me and kicks off her shoes. "Come, you want to take a nap. I can tell your fucking drained."

"Yeah. It's been a long day." I curl up next to her and we cuddle as I slowly drift off to sleep.

I might not have been enough for Mason, but at least I know his sister will always be there for me. I'm thankful for the little things.

CHAPTER 16

YANG

Archer has been on and off the phone with as many people as he can to try and figure out who these Drift Demons are. We get a small break though when we call Wire and Roth happens to be with him. Of course, the ex-villain would know a little something about Bull.

According to him, Bull was part of a different club in Hawaii of all places. They'd got into some really bad shit and they had to get out of dodge. If it was the same people that Roth knew, then Bull is nothing but muscle for hire. He's bad news, but not loyal to anyone except the person who pays him.

It didn't tell us much about who actually took the time out of their day to hire him, but at least we knew for sure that he wasn't someone who was set on trying to build himself a new empire here. I should have known just from how he acted that Bull wasn't someone who thought about long term plans. He was someone who wanted what he wanted right then and there. He thought fucking humiliation and fucking shock value would be enough for us to just give up when we were low and bow down to him. That shit wasn't going to happen not now, not fucking ever.

Archer felt good knowing that it was more than just Bull coming for us. He was focusing on who else in the area would be dumb enough to come for us. Of course, everyone's thinking came right back to René. I didn't want to believe it, but the more shit like this kept happening the easier it was to believe. If we were dealing with René again, we had more than a small problem on our hands. Either way I wish I could just know what the fuck was going on one way or another so we can figure out what the next step is. Right now, everything is up in the air and that is not how I like to live my life.

After the second visit from Ice, I stay in my room and hope that sleep visits me quickly, just like everything else from the day I don't get my way. I just stare at the ceiling, my door open, just in case something goes down and the boys call out for me. I want to be on point for them, but in the same regard I need to get alright with me. I don't think that I am right now. I don't remember the last time I have ever felt so off kilter and to know that it was my sister's best friend that has me all-in knots like this. It's fucking crazy.

The door opens and just like I've been doing since I came into my room I sit up and look out my door to see who is walking in. The last thing I want is for Ice to come back in and walk out again. I don't think I can take it if she does.

It's not Ice who walks in though. It's much fucking worse. I get out of bed and walk towards the door. Christina is there and when she sees me walking up, she comes storming towards me. Fuck she knows.

"Hey, sweetheart. Nice to see you!" Daria says from where she is sitting with Archer.

Christina smiles at her and waves, then focuses her attention right back on me.

"Look I don't know what you were told but ..." It was the last thing I could say before my sister hauls her hand back and smacks the fire out of me.

"Oh shit!" Shyne speaks up and comes out of the kitchen with a bowl of grapes. He could see what was happening from the small cutout that let us look inside the kitchen, but he must have wanted a front row seat to what was going on.

"You dumb fuck!" Christina screams at me.

"Don't put your fucking hands on me again." I growl at her. She was my sister so I didn't want to hurt her, but I would shake her up a little if I had to. I wasn't going to tolerate her disrespecting me even if she was mad about something I had done to one of her friends.

"You unimaginable bastard, what is actually wrong with you? I mean I know mom must have dropped you a few times, but I never thought that you were this fucking dumb." She puts her finger in my chest and pushes me.

"Hey stop your shit!" I bellow at her.

"Oh, fuck you and your intimidation shit. That doesn't work on me Mason, or Yang or whatever the fuck you go by here. You fucked up and you know you did." She glares at me and moves even closer into my space. My sister and I were cut of the same fucking cloth. There was nothing that I could do that would back her down right now apart from whooping her ass and that's not something I really wanted to do.

"I know," I suck my teeth and grab her arm, "Just come on." I tow her to my room so I can get out of earshot of everyone else in the club. If I were going to confess to how much of an asshole I really was, I would rather none of them actually know about it.

I lead her into the room and slam the door behind her.

She opens her mouth the moment I do, but I shut her up immediately. "Christina, I am going to tell you this once and once only. Never again will you walk in this place and embarrass me like that. You're mad or you're upset, whatever it is I can understand, but along with this being my family this is also my fucking job. Don't forget who the fuck is older in this situation. If you do it again, we are going to have a goddamn problem."

She stares at me for a few more seconds before she throws her hands up in surrender. "Fine, I guess I should have slapped you behind the door and not in front of them, but still it doesn't mean that I take it back. You're dead wrong Mason."

"I take it she told you what happened."

"More like she broke down crying her fucking heart out on my shoulder."

I clench my fists and force myself to think about the pain that I must have caused her. Just one more reason to stay away. I'm no fucking good for her. I can't be with someone who is as pure as she is. I'll just dirty her up.

"I know, I'm sorry. I really am. I won't come over for a

while if you think that is best. I know she never wants to see me again and I can respect that. I didn't do it to hurt her or you for that matter. I regret it with every ounce of my being, but we can't go back now. All I can do is try my hardest to give her the space that she needs." I sit on the bed and accept my own words.

"Yeah, I doubt that." She scoffs and sits down next to me. "Let me ask you something Mason, be real with me. Either way I'm not going to say anything to her. Blood oath." She puts her index finger up and I press mine to hers.

When she was a young kid anytime I did something that I wasn't supposed to do I would tell her to take a blood oath that she wouldn't tell our parents. I would put my finger up so we could touch digits as a sort of signature. The blood coursing through her fingers is the same coursing through mine. Now anytime something was serious or we wanted a secret that only the two of us would know we would do this.

"What do you want to know?"

"Did you fuck her just because you wanted to take her virginity? Was this some kind of novelty for you?"

"No, Chris, I didn't even remember that she was still a fucking virgin until she reminded me last night. This wasn't just a novelty for me." I didn't say anymore, I hope she can read through the fucking lines. I have feelings for Ice even if I know I shouldn't.

"Yeah, I didn't think so. Even you fucking that girl earlier today isn't going to keep Isley away from you. The girl is in love with you Mason. As your sister I'm telling you this so you can make the right choice. She's been in love with you for a long fucking time and is only now getting the courage to do something about it. What you do with this information is on you, but I promise you I will kick your ass if you keep making my friend cry." She stands up from the bed and my mind is still stuck after hearing her say that Ice is in love with me. I knew she had a crush, but love? Surely not. There was one other thing that bothers me though.

"She thinks I had sex with that girl from earlier?"

"Yeah, Isley said she saw her on your lap writhing around and kissing your neck. That you were really enjoying it." Christina scowls at me.

"I didn't fuck that girl. Those smiles were forced." I turn away, she is probably the only one who would believe me besides maybe Shyne and Bones after they saw me today, "She was tickling me."

"Oh, shut up." Christina leans her head to the side and a large smile breaks on her face, "You serious, that's what she walked in on?" She laughs and slaps a hand to her thigh. "I can't wait to tell her that she's got it all wrong. I'm sure she'll feel much better about that after I tell her."

"No!" I get up, "Don't say a word to her about it. Let her think what she wants to think."

"But what about what I just said?"

"She may think she's in love with me, but she isn't. She can't fucking be. You know me Chris, you know more about me than anyone and you know someone like Ice doesn't belong with me."

Recognition dawns on her face, she knows what I'm referring to. "Mason when are you going to stop blaming yourself for that. You did nothing wrong. You were deployed, there was nothing that you could have done."

"Yeah, I know that, but it doesn't change who I am or what I will do. It doesn't change what I did after. Just leave it ok. Swear to me that you'll just leave this alone." I wait for her answer and when she nods her head yes, I pull her into a hug and let her go. "Get home safe, you hear me."

"I will, be good." She smiles at me and walks out. I don't worry about anyone in the club messing with her. They all know she's family.

I lay back on the bed and go over what she'd said to me. How Ice had thought that I was fucking Twig, how she supposedly loves me, how she isn't going to stay away from me. I hope the last one isn't true, because I don't think I have the will power to keep pushing her away.

CHAPTER

YANG

Three more days have gone by and Ice has shown up twice. Each time one of my brothers has stopped her at the door. Finally, they were getting the fucking clue that anytime she showed up I lost my shit. The last time she'd shown up, Shyne came back and told me that she looked like she was going to cry when he sent her away. I brush it off, telling him that she always cries and that she'd win an Oscar one day. On the inside I was breaking apart. I was tired of hurting her. Being with her would hurt her and being without her is hurting her. Ever since we had sex it feels like there is nothing I can do that will make things right. I'm hoping time and space is the key. They say time heals all wounds. Except the way this shit hurts right now, I know I'm going to have to be away from her for a long time before this heals.

I lay up at all hours of the fucking night, tense as fuck, waiting for the other shoe to drop from someone. We haven't heard from Bull and I haven't been able to shake Ice. We still don't know who is stealing from the casino and caused the pick up to be short. Everything appears so fucking open ended right now. Archer didn't want us to go on lockdown yet since we had just gotten off one. Only I could tell that Jameson is just chomping at the bit to get Celine and her father locked up in here. Every time she leaves to do anything he is a fucking mess until she gets back. Most times I would have been able to calm him down on my own, but I can't even calm myself down right now.

It's near three in the morning and for the most part the club is pretty silent. Pirate and Shyne are off to get the pick up for the night, while Clay and Bones are on watch. Since the incident with the letter Clay has been walking on fucking eggshells. I feel bad for him, but a little scare is good for him. If he wants to be one of us, he needs to respect the club and his job. There is no mistaking that. This club is a brotherhood, but if we don't all do our fucking part this shit falls to pieces.

It's in the truly serene moments that disaster strikes.

RRRRING

The club phone goes off, at three in the morning it can't be anything good. I hop out of bed and rush to the bar where it goes off again. Clay and Bones rush over to it too, but I get to it first.

"Yeah." I answer right away.

"Fuck, move Shyne! Move your ass!" I hear Pirate screaming on the line, but he isn't talking to me yet.

"God damn it, Pirate! Talk to me!" I try to get his attention, "Clay get Archer right the fuck now."

He runs off and I hear Pirate yelling at Shyne again. I don't know what is going on, but they are in trouble. "Pirate!"

"Yang! We need help, right now. They got us fucking

cornered out here. Hurry the fuck up we can't hold them back for much longer. Shyne, we can't fucking stay here!"

"Copy, we are on the way, are you still on the main road?"

"No, the fuckers ran us off. We're on foot in the fucking swamp. This shit is flooded. The only thing that is keeping them back right now are the fucking alligators."

"Oh shit! Mother fucker!" I hear Shyne scream through the phone and three loud pops echo.

'What the fuck is that!"

"Fucking gator man. Hurry up Yang, this ain't the fucking way to go out." Pirate grunts out.

"Don't say that shit. No one's fucking going out."

Archer runs up to the bar with Jameson and Lex right behind him.

"What the fuck is going on?" Archer asks.

"Something is going down with Shyne and Pirate. They're in trouble, bad." Bones delivers the news to Archer.

"Speaker that now." Jameson orders.

I do.

"We're on the south fucking side not far off the road. We can't go back." Pirate continues.

"Why not? Where are the demons?"

"They right fucking there. Every time we pop our fucking heads up, they got their sights on us. Either we going to get fucking shot or we going to get eaten. I lost the ..." His phone drops. I hear it clatter on the ground then I hear Shyne screaming for him to hold on. Gunshots go off and then the line goes dead.

"Fuck! We have to move! Now!" Archer orders, but

everyone is already running towards the bikes. The roads are still slick, but there is no way that we would all fit in the truck.

"Clay, you protect our fucking home. You understand!" I stare him down as I run out. "Lex let's go."

I know it's fucked up to show one prospect more attention than the other, but I knew for sure that Lex knew how to fucking handle himself. Clay was still a bit soft.

The ride down to the small swamp off the back end of our land is about six minutes away. I don't know why they would have come this way. Despite that, I'm assuming it had something to do with Bull and his bastards trying to gun them all down. I would fucking kill that bastard if he did something to one of my brothers. The swamp is usually pretty low and the gators tend to stay to themselves. Except anytime it really pours, it floods and they like to roam free. If they were stuck in there, it wouldn't be long before one of them thought Shyne or Pirate was dinner. We roll up and the four cars that are there race away. They must not have been expecting us to come for our men. That's not how we roll, when one of us is down than all of us rally. Jameson and Bones are the ones that go into the swamp first. I stay back with Archer and watch for anyone trying to sneak up behind us.

Within a few seconds Shyne runs out while Jameson and Bones have to help a bleeding Pirate.

"What the fuck happened?"

"A motherfucking gator took a chomp at him. This big fucker over here was too fat for even the alligator to get down." Shyne jokes and claps his brother on the back.

"Shut the hell up, I think I've heard enough of you screaming for a lifetime." Pirate looks over to Archer, "Prez, I lost the drop. It's in the fucking swamp somewhere. It fell when we were on the goddamn run."

"Don't fucking worry about that shit right now. Let's get the hell back home and regroup." He pulls Pirate in. "Can you ride?"

"Yeah, I'm good." I rush down the steep decline and help roll both of their bikes up. This must be where they'd ran them off the road. Its lucky the Demons didn't do more damage or Pirate and Shyne could have broken their necks.

A loud whizz goes by my ear the second I bend down to engage the stand.

"Shots!" Archer calls out.

We'd thought the motherfuckers left, but they only went into fucking hiding. All of us were in their line of sight. Pirate though in pain, hops onto his bike and takes off. He is no good to us right now and he knows it. The rest of us get on our bikes and pull away right behind him. I pull my piece out and start shooting the second a low rider mustang pulls in behind me. "Where the fuck are they coming from?" Shyne screams at me from his bike. None of us had time to initiate our in helmet communications so we would have to settle for screaming at each other.

"I don't fucking know … The trees!" I yell back.

The mustang behind me drops back a bit when I'd started shooting, but now he was right on my ass again. We needed to haul ass and get the fuck off the road. It's early in the morning, but that didn't mean we would be alone for long.

Four cars were behind us and only one person had shot at us. I try to find the shooter and take them out. Though between worrying about my bike staying upright and making sure Pirate stays on his all while still trying to outrun them was proving to be impossible. The guy was so close on my ass the tread on my fucking tires was brushing against his bumper, I had no shot.

"Get back to the clubhouse. We'll hunker down there and get rid of these mother fuckers." Archer calls out in front of us. Between all the engines roaring and the wind blowing by my face it's almost impossible to hear anything, but I know for sure that we aren't equipped to deal with these bastards here on the road. Getting back to the clubhouse is the best choice.

Four minutes. It only takes four minutes for us to get back onto our land. It's desolate and flat for the most part, but there is only one dirt road. We can all fit on it, but the big cars behind us don't have the same luck. I look toward the front of the clubhouse, even if we make it inside, they would be on our ass in an instant. This was going to be a bloody fucking fight.

I see Clay at the front door and he is waving us in like a mad man. Signaling that we need to go faster. We are going as fast as we can. He makes the military signal to break off and since most of us here knows what that means we almost instinctively follow instructions. Instead of coming straight in we make a Y and veer to the sides. The second we are clear a deafening blast erupts from behind us. I'm thrown off my bike and two out of the four cars that were chasing us are now flipped up and warped. Huge dark flames are licking up to the sky as the drivers and passengers all burn inside them. Jameson is the closest to me. I rush to pick him up as I open and close my jaw to get the high-pitched ringing in my ears to stop.

"What the fuck? What the hell was that?" Jameson calls out.

"Fucking Clay! That's what I'm fucking talking about!" Shyne pumps his hand in the air. This was Clay. The fucking explosive expert had somehow lined the entrance to the club- house with a bomb of some sort and basically just saved our asses. The two other cars that were chasing us down decide that's the perfect fucking time to get the fuck out of there. It was fine when they were trying to run us over, but now that we were blowing motherfuckers up, they didn't want to play anymore.

When I look around, I see all of my brothers up and moving. Even Pirate is making his way to the clubhouse, he's limping and in pain, but he's still on the move.

Clay runs over to us and helps Pirate. His head turns to Archer, "I'm sorry I tried to call you, but I couldn't get through."

"Don't fucking apologize, you probably just saved our ass." Archer claps him on the shoulder once before he rushes into the clubhouse. We needed to be prepared and he had a lot to get done before anything more happened.

I catch up to Clay and Pirate. "Hey, what the hell convinced you to do that shit?"

"You told me to protect the house. I'd blow up the fucking

world before I let anyone come in here and hurt us." He holds my gaze until he and Pirate moves by. He may not be as strong as Lex, but he was certainly someone we needed on our fucking team.

"God damn it." My head falls back when I take a step into the clubhouse and hear the phone ringing. Never a good fucking thing.

Bones is the one to run over and answer it.

"Speak."

I don't know what is going on, but from the way his face drops I know we have more problems.

"Pirate!" Bones calls out. "It's Capri."

The air gets thick and the commotion dies down a bit. Capri was Pirate's kid sister. He loves her more than life itself. So, if something bad happens to her I don't think any of us would be able to stop him from getting revenge on whoever hurt her.

He hobbles over to the bar, quicker than he's been moving.

I want to know that she's okay, but there was still shit to be done right now. Protocol to fucking follow. Rules to obey.

"Shyne, you and Lex go check the perimeter. Keep in fucking contact if you see anyone lurking around don't be a fucking hero. If you can't drop them right away get us. Clay, any other boom sticks out there we need to know about?" He nods his head yes.

"You need to round them up, carefully. The last thing we need right now is that shit going off under one of our feet." I direct him.

I walk up to Jameson who is busy dragging every gun we

have out of the storage area. He's ready to ride off in the middle of the night and just shoot anyone who is in a fucking car. I know he understands what needs to happen, but I don't know if in all the commotion he is thinking straight. Before everyone loses their fucking heads completely, we need to regroup and pinpoint the next fucking steps. "We need church, got to calm this shit down and get our business in order. If we want to find them and retaliate, we can't just wing it. That's not how this goes."

"You think we should just let those bastards fucking live after the shit they pulled. Pirate could be fucking dead. They could have made it into our home and killed our family. No, they don't get to fucking live." Jameson growls out.

I'm only the SAA and don't override Jameson since he is the VP, but I can advise him. Jameson is only seeing red right now. I might be the only calm that anyone here can count on. "I hear you, bro, but we have to fucking prepare. You know I'm right." I will him to see it my way.

"I'll wait on Archer. If he says we fucking roll, we roll."

I nod my head and look towards Archer's room. The door is open and I see him on the phone with whomever. Probably the doc to get him over here to tend to Pirate. I don't know how bad he's hurt, but getting bit by a fucking alligator can't be fucking fun.

"I'm coming just fucking sit tight." I hear Pirate behind me. He's loud and agitated. He slams down the phone and then bangs his fist down on the bar.

"Hey where are you going?" I ask him when he tries to walk towards the door.

"I got to go. Fuck I got to get Capri." He's wobbling all over the place, the adrenaline and the injuries finally catching up with him.

"What's going on? Is she hurt?" Bones asks.

"No. The motherfuckers lit her fucking bar on fire."

What the fuck? Shit had just taken a turn for the worst. They weren't just coming for us. Bull and his boys were coming for our families. Now fucking heads were going to roll.

"Shit! Did she get out alright?"

He nods his head, but I can see Pirate is going down.

"Let me get her." Bones offers up.

"Nah ... I need ..."

"Brother, you won't make it. We both know it. Let me get her and make sure she's safe." Bones urges Pirate.

Pirate nods his head again and I have to catch him as he all but keels over right next to me. Bones races out and I hear his bike tearing down the road. Lex and Shyne come back in at that very moment, "Lex, Shyne, you two follow behind Bones. Watch his back."

"What's going on?" Shyne asks, but is already backing out the door.

"He's getting Capri. They burned her bar down." Anger clouds Shyne's face for a second before he turns and runs to get on his bike. Lex does the same.

In all of thirty minutes our entire fucking world had exploded. Clay comes back in with a small device that looks to be disconnected. Archer and Jameson are talking while Pirate is barely conscious hanging on my arms.

Daria and Celine come out to help with Pirate. The rest of us go to church and take a breath, even if it's just for a second.

Archer jumps straight into it the second everyone is in their seats. "Do we know for sure that it was the Drift Demons that fucked with Capri?"

"Who the hell else do you think it is? We've let these bastards go on the loose for too long. We need to fucking end them tonight." Jameson seethes.

"Even if we don't go looking for them right now. I think it's time for a lockdown." I speak my peace, too much shit was going on and there were too many of us on the move.

"On a lockdown from who? Did you see who was in those cars tonight, because I did." Archer barks.

"What are you talking about?" Jameson asks.

"I know from Roth that the Drift Demons are only 8 drivers strong, including Bull. He likes to keep shit small so he doesn't have to split the pay too many ways."

I heard that tidbit of information, but I didn't know how that mattered to us right now. Did he think that just because there were only a few of them that they wouldn't be deadly? There weren't many of us either.

"I still don't get it Archer. Why are we holding off on this shit? We need to just go find the rest of them and kill them." Jameson jumps up from his chair, but Archer doesn't move. That severe glare that he gets in his eyes just as he is about to go the fuck off usually puts people in their place. It does with Jameson now.

Instead of screaming back at Jameson like most would do Archer simply talks. "I think you may have forgotten what the fuck your kutte says. You are the VP of this chapter; I am the president. If I say that we sit back and let them burn the fucking town down, that is what the hell we will do. My word is fucking law and if you're all of a sudden not down with that, leave your fucking rags on my table and get the fuck out."

Jameson's hands clench into fists and he stares at Archer for a second before he sits back down in his chair. His face turns a deep red and his whole body looks more tense than I'd ever seen it. Jameson would do anything for Archer and this club. I don't ever remember a time that Archer had to threaten to disband him.

"Now, back to what the hell I was saying." Archer leans forward, "There are only 8 members of the Drift Demons. There were 8 of them in the cars that were chasing us tonight. How the fuck are they here chasing us and downtown at Capri's lighting it on fire? Go into lockdown and we don't even know who the hell we are hiding from. Jameson is right, we need to take these bastards the fuck out. But we need to know who the hell our enemy is first. Lockdown is coming, but I need everyone out getting me the information to get this shit under control. First things first, once everyone is back, I want all of you to organize well checks on your families and our allies. Clay took out a chunk of Bull's men so he may get desperate and fuck up. We need to find out for sure who burned down Capri's place. Maybe we find out once and for all who is bank rolling Bull. End this shit." Archer looks to Jameson and then me. "Get the hell out of here. Y'all know what to do."

My mind is a buzzing mess and I feel like I'm putting out fires, but never really fixing any of the problems.

One thing at a time. First step is what?

I exhale and find that one kernel of peace in my mind. We were all together. We would all be okay if we managed to keep everyone on alert and out of harm's way.

CHAPTER

18

YANG

The next day, we have to call in a fucking tow truck to get the burned cars off our lawn. We've used them before so they don't ask any questions about the drivers or why they see what looks like blood. We pay them and the burnt cars are taken away.

Capri came to stay with us last night. There was nothing that could be salvaged from the fire, but she did confirm one point that Archer had made. The fire was started by someone at the same time that Bull and his cronies were chasing Pirate and Shyne from the casino which was on the other side of town. There is no way that they could have been there and at Capri's bar. The pyro had to be someone else.

Pirate was in bad shape, apparently the gator had clamped down pretty hard. Even though it didn't rip off any of his limbs the force of his jaw and the germs in the dirty swamp water had given Pirate a hell of an infection in his leg. The doc had to cut pieces of his thigh off that had died already. His midsection was severely bruised, but luckily there were no puncture wounds there and no internal bleeding. As long as we got the infection in his leg under control Pirate would be just fine. The issue is he didn't want to stay in bed. He was only concerned with Capri and getting revenge on whoever did this to her. She stayed in the room with him all night crying and curled into his chest.

I grab my stuff and knock on the door to Archer's room. He is holding Daria, but still calls me in. "What's up?"

"School should be over by now, I'm going to go down to the dorms and check on Christina. Make sure her place is secure and all that. Tell her that she may have to get some things together and stay with us if things don't die down."

"Are you sure she's going to go for that? You know she's not a fan of the club. She's never come for lockdowns before."

I shake my head at how fucking stubborn my sister can be. Since I've been a Wing, we've had three lockdowns and she's never come to even one of them. She claims that her living among all the college kids is enough protection and that no one is looking for her anyway. People barely know she exists.

"I'm hoping she will change her mind this time. It's almost time for break, so there won't be too many kids around."

"Are you sure you aren't hoping that you'll get the other one to come with her."

"Ahh, I don't think she will come at all."

"You want her to be safe though. I know that much." Archer says.

"I do. Definitely."

He shakes his head before he continues. He kisses Daria's head and walks over to me, "Yang, level with me for a minute, because I'm a little miffed by that whole situation. Why are you fighting so hard against what is obvious to everyone else? Yeah, she's young, but it's not illegal."

I didn't want to get into it, but maybe I need to in order to move on and get back to normal. Maybe I was still so fucking off the wall, because I was keeping this shit bottled inside.

"Did you know both of my parents died about two years before I got here?"

"No, I didn't. I'm sorry to hear that."

"Yeah, it was a home invasion. Two bastards came into their house, stole everything they could get their hands on and then lit my house on fire. The fire department managed to get the fire under control but my parents were inside and were killed. Thankfully, my sister was at a friend's house when all of this happened. I remember her calling me. Instead of crying with her on the phone or getting irate. I just started to plan what I would do next. The culprits were caught and plead guilty to a lesser charge. They were placed in rehab and then a psychiatric ward, but they were home on house arrest a year later. Because they were minors when they committed the crime, it was like a slap on the wrist for them. Though in my heart justice had not been served. I knew what the plan was. My next steps were already planned out. I didn't even mourn my parents' deaths correctly. I got my leave, got my alibi together, did my research and found out who it was that came into my home, the ones that had destroyed my life. And I killed them. I killed them and their families. The two twin brothers were sixteen years old on a bender looking for drug money when they'd committed the crime. They were having their eighteenth birthday party when I walked in their house and killed them all. I killed those two eighteen year old kids, their parents, an uncle, a cousin, and even one godparent. That night I slept like a baby in one of their beds. And the next morning I chopped them up and dumped all of their remains in the swamp. It didn't even turn my stomach as I watched a hand sink below the surface and get torn to shreds by one of the gators."

Archer didn't show any emotion on his face. I had basically just admitted to a mass killing spree, something that only my sister knew about. If that didn't say how much I trusted this man I don't know what would.

"I came home, washed up, and watched TV." I close my eyes not wanting to see the acceptance he may give me or the judgement either. "You have to be someone completely devoid of a fucking soul to do the shit that I've done and sleep without a care in the world. I'm not right, she doesn't deserve to be with someone like me. Fuck, no one deserves to be with someone like me. If I can be so numb to something like that, there is no way that I can expect anything good to come to me. That's just not meant for me. I'm not for her."

"Your demons are a part of who you are, but they are not all of you." Archer speaks the second I'm done. "We've all done some fucked up shit and there is always someone who can see through the monsters and devils that run rampant inside of us to the good that we are. If I didn't know any better, I think this Isley might just be the one who can see through to the real you." He doesn't dwell, but moves away not even acknowledging the fact that I had just confessed to murder. He was still trying to get me to see that I wasn't just some fucking psychopath. Too bad I don't believe him.

As I ride to Christina's apartment, I'm super nervous. My gut rolls as I get closer to her place. What the fuck do I say to Ice? She lives there too. Hey, how you doing? Sorry I haven't talked to you since we fucked. I almost regret not telling Lex or Clay to come over here and check on them for me. When I park up, I'm surprised that I don't see Isley's car right away. I go upstairs and knock on the door. Christina swings it open straight away without even checking to see who it is. I hate that she doesn't take her safety more serious.

"Mason, what are you doing here?"

"I came here to check on you. Everything alright?" My eyes scan the place, but I don't hear or see anyone else.

"Yes." Her S -sound lingers in the air.

"Good. Good." I lean to see behind her in the kitchen, but Ice isn't in there either.

"You know you could have just said you came here to see my best friend, my feelings are hurt either way."

My face snaps to hers, "I did not." I blurt out.

"Sure!" she laughs and steps aside to let me in. "She's not here anyway."

I run my hand through my hair, relaxing a bit, but mildly disappointed that I won't get to see her. "Listen for real, there are some bad things going on with my club. I know you don't like it, but I may need you to come stay with me for a little while."

"Ugh, no. I don't need to do that. You always come here telling me about something big and bad that's happening, but nothing ever does. I'll be fine here." She complains and stomps away.

"Christina, stop!" I give her the full big brother treatment. "You're all I have in the world and unfortunately my life is full of big and bad things. I don't want it to spill over onto you. If this gets much worse, you're coming to stay with me until it's over. No more push back you understand."

"You can't force me to go there?"

"Fine would you prefer me come here? Be vulnerable and out in the open? So, they can come here and kill me before killing you too anyway?"

"That's not fair. Don't do that to me." She puts her hands on her hips.

"I don't want to do anything to you, but I need you to stop always fighting me on this. I'm not trying to be all up in your business or stop you from living your life. I just need you to be safe."

She sighs and wraps her arms around my midsection while she presses her head to my chest. I used to push her off when she would hug me, but today I revel in the feeling. "I love you too big bro." She lets me go and looks around. "It's not now though, right?"

"No not yet, but it may be coming soon so just be ready. In the meantime, you really got to do something more about the security you have here."

"What security?"

I laugh at her, "That's the fucking problem." Over the next hour or so I go over a few things at her place. She shows me her fire escape and it actually is pretty hidden. You wouldn't even know it was there if you weren't looking for it. Her name wasn't listed on the buzzer key downstairs. She promised to verify who was at the door before she opened it anytime someone comes. I also hid a few weapons around the house for her just in case. A knife here and there, no guns since she'd never learned how to shoot. Now at least if someone barged in, she would be able to get her hands on a weapon right away to protect herself.

By about five I'm leaving and going back to the club. Christina promises to be available whenever I call and that's all I can really ask for right now. I get on my bike and roll out. As I turn to get on the road that leads me home, I see Isley walking down the street with a short jean skirt on, a loose sweater and knee-high combat boots. She is looking down at her phone and doesn't even realize that I'm right there. She is walking the back way home. I wonder if Christina had told her that I just left? Either way it was getting dark and I wasn't about to let her walk home wearing that. It was about a mile back to my sister's house. Nope there is no way.

I rev my bike and stop directly in front of her.

She jumps and almost drops her phone when my bike appears in her view.

"What the fuck!" She lifts her head and one tear falls down her face before she places a hand on her chest and closes her eyes.

"Where the hell are you going?" My voice is gruff.

She drops her hand down and opens her eyes. Her face tries to break into a smile, but almost as if she'd just remembered what had happened between us it turns into a scowl. "None of your business."

"Where's your car?"

"Again, same answer." She continues to walk now moving further from the street and away from me on the bike.

"Ice!" I call out to her, but she continues to ignore me. I turn off my bike and run on foot to catch her. "Where are you going?"

"I'm going home, God, now move." I don't and she lifts her head all the way up to stare at me. "Please." Those bright blue eyes hypnotize me.

I shake myself out of it and grab her elbow, "Come on, I'm going to take you there. You don't need to be walking all the way back."

"No, I'm not going with you. I'd rather walk a hundred miles than go anywhere with you right now."

"This isn't a request, Ice. Come on." I tug her again, but she rips her arm away from me this time and turns to look around.

"What are you looking for?"

"Your girlfriend, you remember the one you were all snuggled up with on the couch. She must be who you're talking to right now, because if I recall correctly and I know I do, you told me that you didn't want anything to do with me."

"I never said that Isley, never."

"You said you regretted being with me."

I can't bring myself to tell her that I don't. I don't want to get her hopes up that maybe there is something more than what happened to come. That night is all there will ever be even though my cock is harder than fucking diamonds right now. All I can think about besides getting her home is how bad I want to shove my tongue down her throat. Better yet, shove my tongue in that tight pussy.

"She's not my girlfriend." It's the only consolation I can give her right now.

"Oh great, your fuck buddy. What does it matter?"

"She's not my fuck buddy either. We weren't fucking. What you saw was them fucking with me." I explain to her.

"What does that even mean?" she crosses her arms over her chest, but at least now she isn't walking away.

"Did you see the two other men standing right there laughing their heads off?"

She looks away for a second before she nods her head yes, "It's because they were making fun of me. She was tickling me and they've never seen a grown man that was ticklish."

"You're lying." She squints at me before one corner of her mouth goes up slightly, "You can't be that ticklish. Are you serious?"

"Yeah, I don't know why it didn't go away when I was a kid, but it's not something I go around boasting to everyone. She was trying to cheer me up and happened to tickle my neck. It was downhill from there."

She shakes her head again, "Sorry, I'm going to have to fact check this, because if that were the case you would have said so. It's been days of you letting me think what I saw was something different." She looks down at her phone, swipes at the screen, and puts the call on speaker. My sister picks up on the third ring.

"Yoooo."

"Hey boo, got a question for you." Ice looks up in my face waiting for me to take back what I said. I don't, instead I focus in on her face. She must have been out in the sun recently, her freckles are more pronounced. She has a few on each cheek and four on her nose. I'd counted them one time.

"Do I have the answer?" My sister says warily.

"Yup, but you have to swear to tell the truth."

"Yeah, always."

"Is your brother ticklish?"

"Fuck." Christina moans out. "Wait, is he there?"

"Yeah."

"Oh, ok then. Yes! He's so fucking ticklish its absolutely fucking adorable. Get him on his neck. Like near his ear … oh and his left side is way more ticklish than his right."

"What the fuck. It was a simple yes or no question! You don't need to give her fucking directions" I yell at her through the phone.

She laughs on the other end, "Oh and if you get his legs, his thighs and knees! He gave me five dollars once, because I cornered him and tickled the hell out of him." Christina's cackling like a fucking hyena on the other end, Ice is doing the same here.

I remember the day Christina got the five dollars out of me. She'd almost killed me. I was under my fucking car working on shit when she came and sat on my legs. I couldn't get out without hurting her or me and she'd used that to her advantage. She tortured the hell out of me.

"I'm going to come back and fuck you up." I threaten my sister when Ice expertly gets her hands against my neck and starts tickling me.

"No! Fuck no! I'm not playing with you Ice." I back up from her. I can easily outrun her, out muscle her, and every-thing in between. Except this is the first time in days that I'm feeling free and at ease. She's laughing and I'm laughing. It feels normal.

The phone is clicked off and she steps in front of me to tickle my left side just like Christina had told her. I laugh loud as I push her away, careful not to push too hard and hurt her. She goes in with both hands now tickling my neck and my side. Now it's too much. I grab her and turn her so she is facing away from me. I pull her so her back is flush with my front. "Stop playing with me Ice." I growl in her ear. She gasps and sinks further into my grasp. We are both out of breath and every fucking ounce of me wants her. I need her, but I know I don't deserve her. I know if she were to be with me it would be a disservice to her.

"Why didn't you tell me? Why didn't you tell me that she wasn't with you like that? Do you just like hurting me now that you know you can?"

It's like a slap in the face and to my sex drive. "No, I don't ever want to hurt you. You know that." Enough is enough, I need to get back to the clubhouse and she needs to get home. "Look this doesn't mean anything, there's no reason to even talk about it. Let's go so I can get you home. "

"I can get home on my own Mason." Her words are like acid. She turns away, her long hair flipping in the wind with the motion.

Fine, guess I have to do this the old fashioned way. I grab her around her waist and lift her off the ground.

"Hey! Stop! What the hell are you doing Mason?" She yells at me as I walk her over to my bike and sit her down on the front. I'm sure if I try to sit her on the back she'd just jump off. I sit behind her and close her in with my arms on the handlebars.

"Oh, you asshole!"

"You already knew that Ice." I say in her ear.

"No, I thought I knew you, Mason. But it's obvious I know much less than I thought I did."

I pull out slowly, but she squirms in front of me and I have to go at a snail's pace, "What the hell Ice, why are you being so difficult about this?"

"Me! It's not me who's being difficult." She turns her head so she can talk to me. "You feel something for me Mason. I know you do. I see it in your eyes. I felt it in the way you kissed me. You feel something, but you don't want to admit it. You won't tell me why either."

On the inside I'm raging against myself. I want to say fuck the world and even her future happiness, to take her. She keeps offering herself up. I'm not strong enough to keep denying myself.

"You're wrong Ice. I don't. That's why I'm not going any further. I don't feel anything." Even as those fucked up lies leave my mouth, I know she doesn't believe me. I need to at least follow it up with something real, "You need to be with someone more like you. Someone close to your age."

"You know what Mason. I'm so tired of hearing you say that. So sick of you just trying to play everything off like I'm some helpless girl who doesn't know what I'm doing or what I want. Do you think I can't get a man my own age or that I would somehow miraculously be more attracted to someone I went to school with?" She turns to face front, but she moves back so she is leaning on me. I keep my hands on the handle-bars, but I am having a hard time completely focusing on the road in front of me especially when she is so close. I am grateful that the route we are on is mostly backroads and service roads.

"You think that when I walked into that clubhouse the other day, I didn't already know the choice I was making. I chose you Mason. I still choose you. I'm not going to want someone else just cause we share the same birthday or because we may watch the same shows." Her hand snakes behind her back and before I know what's happening, she is stroking my cock through my jeans.

"Fuck. Isley ... Ice, stop."

"No, you want this. I know you do. We both do and there's nothing wrong with that." I keep my eyes open, but I slow from the 25 miles per hour that I was doing to barely ten. She shuffles back some more and manages to slide her hand into my pants. I was only wearing a pair of sweatpants so it wasn't very hard. My cock was though.

"Ice you have to fucking stop. Fuck." I scold her again, but I don't move my hands from the handlebars.

"You don't want me to. We're good together Mason. I'm not asking for the world just for you to give it a shot."

"You should." I bend my head and kiss her neck once before I lean back up to focus on the road. "You should ask for and be given the entire fucking world."

"If you let me in that's all I need." She secures her feet on the rests that I put them on and moves back a bit more. "You got me Mason. I know you do." She says and she brings her other hand behind her back to pull my pants out and down so my hard cock is free and pressed into her hand. She brings one hand back to her front to balance herself while she jerks me back and forth with the hand still behind her back.

"Ice, why do you drive me so fucking crazy? You need to listen to me. I can't be with you like that. I can't." I groan out, but I rock my hips into her hand after every stroke.

"That's not what your body says." She jerks me off as hard and fast as she can in this position.

"What are you doing, Isley? My body clenches and my hands tense causing the bike to accelerate slightly. "I'm not fucking playing with you. Stop." I put all the warning I have left into the words.

"You want me to stop, make me Mason." I feel her shuffle back and then quicker than I can react she raises up, lines my cock up with her pussy and slams herself down.

"Fuck! What the fuck! Holy shit! What the fuck!" I curse and my body goes into overdrive as I fight to keep the bike on the desolate road, her on the bike and safe in-between my arms, and my hips from rocketing up from the seat further into her tight pussy.

She arches her back using my thighs to give her leverage as she secures her feet on the front crash bars. She grinds on me hard, barely lifting, but more rocking my dick within her tight walls.

"Mason, this can't feel this good and be wrong."

I look down and her head is all the way back against my shoulder. Her eyes flutter open and a soft smile crosses her face. She swirls and bucks against me.

I'm gasping for breath as my body completely surrenders to her.

"Mason, you want me to stop now?" She digs her nails into my thighs and quickens her motion. I let go of the clutch side of the handlebars to grip her hair. "You like getting me to this point don't you. No, don't fucking stop. I told you before to stop playing with me." She whimpers and hisses, but she begins to bounce a little higher and grind a little harder.

"Ahh Mason, I don't know. Oh God. It's so intense."

She wasn't lying about that. This shit feels so fucking good. It feels too good. I'm going to come hard. I need to get off this bike. I let go of her hair and secure my hand on the handlebars again looking for somewhere to stop. The road we are on is just a service road, but people could still drive by. I see what looks to be a small shipping company. On the side of the building there are stacks of pallets. The doors and windows are shuttered so I don't think anyone is there. I turn my bike off the service road and into the side alleyway where I see the pallets, and park.

"Mason, what are we doing?" She stops moving clearly unsure about where we are. It's a fucking alley.

"Move that ass now." I smack her bare thigh with my hand and she slowly raises off my lap. I quickly hop off my bike and examine the area. It was actually much better than I'd thought. The pallets didn't look too disgusting and they were neatly arranged in a column of stacks. So, if we went in between one of the stacks no one would be able to see us from the street or the front of the building. I push her into a space between two stacks of pallets. I take off five or so making the stack low enough for me to lay her down on. I grab my kutte and put it on the rough wood, it's no down comforter, but it'll have to do.

I push her down and lift her legs so no part of her body is on the wood except for her back and head which is laying on my kutte.

I grab the panties that she had previously pushed to the side and rip them off. I don't have time; I need her so fucking bad right now. She gasps and lets a soft moan. I line up with her pussy and thrust straight in. Her hand juts out to stop me, but I'm already buried to the hilt. I give her no time to adjust. My mind tells me to slow down. Except the wild animal inside of me that she keeps on tempting is telling me not to hold back. She'd asked for this. Constantly. Over and over. She offered herself up on a platter. Logic flies directly out my mind when I knock her hand away and ram into her. I moan loudly and so does she. Sweat is already pricking my back as I race in a full sprint to come.

"Yes … Hard. Fuck me hard Mason." Her deep sultry siren's voice wraps around me and I do exactly what she wants. Her sweater is so big it's covering most of her. I hate that I can't see her.

"Show me those gorgeous tits Ice." I can't be bothered to reach up and do it myself I need to hold her up so I can stay this fucking deep inside of her.

She does what I ask immediately. She pulls the cups of her black bra down and the cool air puckers her nipples. I lean down as best I can without slowing my motion and suck one nipple, followed by the next.

I try to raise up, but she grabs hold of my neck. Keeps me leaned down while she pulls herself up until her face is directly in front of mine. She attacks my mouth, the vicious-ness of it only pushing me to fuck deeper and harder. I'm hurting her. In the back of my mind, I knew there's no way that I wasn't hurting her. She'd be bruised inside by the time I was done. Marked. All fucking mine.

She digs her nails into my back. She stops kissing me abruptly. Her eyes go wide for a second before her eyebrows softly knit together and her mouth drops open in a small O.

"That's it. Come for me baby. Damn it. What are you doing to me?" I groan against her mouth and a deep rumble settles in my chest. Her body squeezes and milks my dick as she climaxes. When she's done her body goes lax as she whim-pers and moans out in bliss.

I can't make her come again now. I'm too far gone. One small spurt of cum pulses out my slit, as if it was overflowing out of me. I groan and snarl as I keep fucking her, feeling the pressure of my eminent release building past an unbearable level. That one small spurt has already set my body on fire. I know how good it already is and I'm stuck there, stuck in ecstasy. An illogical part of me is scared that I will never be able to stop fucking her, because it feels so good. Every stroke makes me feel like I'm coming. Another part of me, hesitant and praying that I can hold on just a little bit longer, knowing that this will be the best orgasm anyone in all the world has ever had. If the amount of euphoria one could feel from orgasming could be measured this shit was about to break records. After what feels like forever, my body can hold back no longer. Just when I think it can't get any better a small voice inside my head reminds me that I don't have a condom on. The thought of her being pumped full of my seed is the final straw. I lean my head back and a thunderous roar comes out my throat. Flames lick down my spine as I explode over and over inside of her. My body jerks forward hard and I gather Ice in my arms, making sure to keep her fully seated on my still spasming dick. My cum leaks out of her even before I pull out.

CHAPTER 19

YANG

The incredible high rolling through my body freefalls dragging me into a deep low.

I fucked up again. What the fuck is wrong with me?

"See I told you."

I pull out of her and cringe when my cum splatters on my boot. "You told me what? Nothing has changed."

Ice sits up and drags her sweater over her breasts, "What the hell are you talking about nothing has changed? We're good together. You see that. Don't you?"

"Ice I'm telling you this, because I do care for you and I do want you to be happy. I'm no good for you. This fucking is just that. Fucking. I'm attracted to you, but there is no way that it can ever be anything more." I reach my hand up to try and touch her cheek, but she pulls away from me.

"Are you insane?"

"Yes." I answer her honestly. After the shit I did to the ones who killed my parents, I would never believe that I was completely sane. No matter what anyone said.

"You know what." She throws her hands up and pushes

me away hard. "Fuck this. I love you, Mason. Maybe more than I should. I know in my soul that we should be together to at least give it a try, but I'm tired of fucking chasing you. I'm tired of trying to force you to see the good thing right in front of your face. If you are too fucking stupid to realize that we fit, I'm not going to force feed this shit to you. You want whatever the fuck we've been doing to stop. So be it. I'm just you're sister's friend now."

Fuck I want to grab her. "You love me?"

"Yeah, I do. Don't worry, I got the picture loud and fucking clear Mason. I'm sure those feelings will go away soon. Maybe Christina was right, I do just need to find some random guy to fuck and get you out of my system."

What the fuck, she's not fucking anyone!

I take a menacing step in her direction and she jumps back slightly, her eyes wide in surprise.

I stuff all my feelings down and take that same step back. She's right, she needs to get me out of her system. It's the only way. If that is what she feels like she needs to do to erase me I can't do anything to stop her.

"Let's go. You need to get off the street."

"Sure." She crosses her arms over her chest and we walk back to my bike. She gets on the front like I had her before. I know I should put her behind me, but I'm being selfish. If this is the last time that I'm going to be able to feel her in my arms I'm going to take it.

I hop on behind her and turn the bike on. After I make sure she is secure I turn the bike around and start on the way back to her and Christina's off campus dorm.

The vibration of the bike flows through me and the feeling of her small body against mine is like the best form of relaxation. I want to get used to this feeling, but I know I can't. I need to just soak up as much of this as I can now. I take an easy pace back to the service road we were on. She didn't say a word to me, her shoulders tense as she leans forward as much as she possibly could to get away from being so close to me. Except she couldn't take away how her hair smells or the way her neck curves or the memories of her head against my shoulder as she bounced up and down on my dick. No matter how mad she was she would never be able to take that away.

"Mason." It almost didn't register to me that she was talking to me until she taps me on the leg.

"Yeah?" I lean down to speak to her.

"You know them?"

"What? Who?"

She points in the side mirror and my eyes follow the gesture. Behind us are two dark cars. That wouldn't bother me except they are obviously tailing me. I'm not going more than fifteen miles per hour so they are creeping at five. On top of that their lights are off, but it's already dark. Those cars are following us.

Oh fuck. Fuck no.

I can't bring her back to the apartment complex now. There is no way out of here and I would not only be directing them to her, but my sister too. I can't believe I put her in such incredible danger. I should have just taken her back to the goddamn apartment when I had the chance, but no, I had to go get my dick wet first. Fucking selfish. The reasons just keep piling on, she doesn't belong in my life.

"Ice, I need you to not freak out, ok? I got you. I'm here."

She turns her head in my direction, I no longer see anger in her face. Now I see the trusting Ice I've always known. "What's wrong?"

"My club is in a bit of shit right now. I don't know for sure, but I think those guys behind us might not be friendly. I'm going to go really fast in a second, I need you to be calm." My voice is almost void of emotion as I explain to her what is going on. I don't want her to know just how fucking dangerous this might be if they are from the Drift Demons. I don't want to admit how dangerous it is to myself.

"Got it, I trust you. Let's go."

Even after all the shit I put her through she still trusts me and I believe her too. I lean forward and kiss the side of her head. I don't care if it's against what I've been telling her. I'm worried and need her to know that I'm here with her.

"Ok, hold on. I promise I know what I'm doing. We will not fall; it'll get scary, but I got you." I grip the handles and once I feel her nod, I twist the throttle and pop the clutch like the fucking professional I am. The bike rockets forward quickly going from the leisurely fifteen miles per hour we were just doing to about forty-five. Just like I suspected the cars behind us speed up too, but as I start taking different maneuvers, they throw their high beams on and try to run us down. I'm blowing down the side roads going about 90 right now and I'm running out of non-populated area. If there was anything to dart out in front of me right now it would be disastrous. When the bike hits a hundred and twenty miles per hour and Ice is hunkered down in front me as low as she can get, I start looking for any possible out that I can take. I would call Archer, but I can't get to my phone. I'm on my own right now. On my own with the one woman, I'd give up my life for than have her sitting in front of me right now.

I take a sharp left and turn onto an abandoned road that I knew turned into dirt. It would be hell on the bike, but I was hoping that like before the cars wouldn't be equipped to handle the same terrain as my bike could. When we roll onto the dirt road, my back tire skids out slightly. Ice screams and digs her hands into my thighs.

"I got you." I scream at her over the roar of the bike and the cars behind us.

She nods, but doesn't let go of my leg.

I steady the bike and push even further onto the unpaved road; small sapling trees and brush are everywhere. Quickly it began to change into dense greenery. I thought for sure that we would be able to lose them in there, but at the final second, right before we could get into the tree line a four by four barrels out in front of us. I have to brake hard. I grab hold of Ice and lock her to my front as my bike pushes up a huge cloud of dust. The wheels lock and skid as it tries to bring us to a stop. We manage to stop a foot or so before impact. We were fucked. Two men came out of the four by four and the two cars that were behind us stop. A man comes out of each of those cars. One of them is Bull.

"Wow, that was exhilarating! Every time I want to talk to you guys, everyone makes it so difficult. I had really hoped that we could be friends, but that doesn't seem to be happening. Such a shame."

"You can be friends with the barrel of my gun if you want." I say as I pull Ice behind me. Her body curling into my back as she trembles and tears stream down her face.

"I'd save the puns if I were you. I'm sure you are going to have a lot to say in a while." Bull walks over to us and grabs for my arm. I yank it away, but one of the men that was in the four by four walks up behind me and grabs Ice.

"Get your fucking hands off of her!" I lunge for the man, but Bull pulls out a gun and presses it to the center of my head. My eyes cross for a second as I look at it. "I don't want to make this messy, but you need to come with me. I found some new friends and wouldn't you know it, they really want to talk to the Wings of Diablo too."

"Fine. I'll go with you. Let her go. She doesn't know anything about anything I was just dropping her off."

"No, I can't do that. She knows who you are and that is enough for me." Bull grabs my arm again. The both of them walk Ice and me to the car. Ice slides in first and I follow. I watch as the other two men take my bike and roll it into the back of the four by four. I had no idea where they were taking us or who Bull's new friends are, but I knew I had to get Ice out of here. Her eyes find mine and like always I expect to see anger or hatred, but instead I see the normal tears and behind that strength.

"You got me, I know it."

I pull her tighter against me. I did have her. I'd always fucking have her.

CHAPTER 20

ICE

How the fuck can one of the best damn days of my life so quickly turn into the worst. Not only did I find out that Mason wasn't fucking with that woman, but we also had passionate sex which I was sure would lead to him admitting his true feelings. That shit didn't happen and the day has just gone from bad to the worst.

Why the fuck didn't I take a cab home or something?

I'm strapped to a chair in a room with Mason right now. He tries for a while to pull himself out of the binds, but they are metal. They have him cuffed at the wrists, ankles, and waist. There is nowhere for him to go. It's amazing how peaceful he gets when he stops trying to get out. I assume he figured out there was no way for him to do it, like he accepted his fate and would live with whatever came next. At first, I thought he was giving up, but I know that's not it. Mason would keep fighting until the end, he just wasn't going to let them see him rattled.

"Are you ok? Are the binds too tight?" He asks me.

"I can't say I'm perfect, but I'm not hurting." I respond, my breath still shaky. I had cried the entire way here, but I was finally starting to settle down. Probably because I knew that Mason was so close.

"Ok. They are probably going to want to get something out of me. I'll tell them, I don't want you to worry about what happens to me ok. If I get them to let you go. I want you to just run until you find somewhere safe."

"What? You think I would just leave you? No, we fight together."

"No Isley, this isn't a fight for you." He lets his head fall back and rolls his shoulders back and forth. "This is the reason. This is why we can't be together. Not because I don't want you, or don't care for you. I have thought about what our life could be if we were together over and over again and it always ends the same. You fighting for me. Fighting for someone who doesn't deserve to have someone as good as you. I'm not good for you. I'm not good for anyone. I need you to see that Ice. Look at me and really see what kind of person I am. I'm not your prince charming, I'm the evil fucking demon that destroys everything in sight without a care in the world."

I shake my head. I don't know what the hell he is talking about or how he got this fucked up idea of himself, but that is not who he is. Besides, it's definitely not something that he can force me to see. "Mason, I'll never see that, because it's not true. Why the hell would you think that about yourself?"

He huffs out an impatient breath, "Ice, you don't know what you're talking about. You don't know me or what I'm capable of. I think this of myself, because I know it's true. I've done some truly fucked up things and I don't feel bad about them. Things I should feel bad about."

"What?" I try to catch his gaze, but he doesn't look back my way, "What things should you feel bad about?"

He still doesn't answer me. I know that he won't. There is one thing that I think he may be talking about, but I've never said it out loud.

"Is it about, the Wellsley boys?" I keep my voice low, because if it's not he's going to be very fucking upset that I would bring them up right now. They'd killed his parents and got off with a slap on the wrist, because of who they knew.

His gaze finally jerks up to mine. A death glare like I've never seen from him before in his eyes. "What are you talking about?"

"We don't have to talk about it. I just want to know if that's why you think this?"

"What do you know about the Wellsley boys?"

I didn't know which way to go with this. "Are you going to hurt me?" The question jerks him out of his daze and he clenches his jaw for a second before he starts to talk.

"Do you think I will?"

"No."

"What do you know about the Wellsley boys?" He asks again.

I keep my eyes locked on his and try to keep things as vague as possible I say, "I know you took care of the problem."

His eyes expand and he starts to breathe faster. He looks

around the room and starts to pull on the restraints again. "She told you. I can't believe she told you. How the fuck could she do that shit to me?" He mutters to himself.

"No, Christina didn't tell me anything."

"How the hell could you know anything if she didn't tell you? I only ever told her, never wrote it down, never was questioned for it. The only way for you to know is if she told you." He barks at me.

"Technically you're the one who told me."

"What are you talking about?"

"You know my parents have never been the greatest human beings on earth, right?" He nods and I continue, "Well somewhere around ninth grade they started to get into trouble more often and Christina started sneaking me in your house. I stayed in her room for a whole summer once and your mom didn't even notice," I laugh as I reminisce about the woman that was taken out of his life far too soon, "You know, she probably did know, but just didn't say anything. Your mom was cool like that. Anyway, anytime there was problems at my house I'd come stay at yours. It got to the point where I didn't even ask. I'd just come over and find someplace to sleep. If it were late, I'd climb through the window so I wouldn't wake anyone. No one ever asked any questions if they woke up in the morning and I came down for breakfast. The night that you came home I'd climbed in through your window and was sleeping in your room. It was my favorite spot, not only would I fantasize about you, but it's where I felt the safest. I had my first experience with self-pleasure right there on your bed." I look up at him with a smile on my face, but he is still just staring at me. "That one night, you came home. I didn't know you were coming or I wouldn't have slept in your room. Christina didn't even know I was there. I heard your voice and I was rushing to get out of your room when I heard what you had said. I heard what you did to those boys and, the rest of them. I left the next morning before Christina ever knew I was there and just never brought it up."

"You knew?" His voice is strangled. His eyes squint as he shakes his head slowly from side to side. "All this time, you knew what I did?"

"Yeah, I didn't think you wanted to talk about it?" I watch him for more of his reaction.

"You don't think it's ... I mean, I murdered them Ice. You don't think there is something wrong with that?"

"Mason, I knew your parents. I loved them. They were the parents I wished I had. I knew the people's lives that they affected. To have them ripped away from us like that was ungodly. You did what needed to be done for you to heal. I don't think you're bad, because of what you did. I think you will do bad things if you need to. Why should you feel bad about what you did? The next day, after I knew everything, there was not one ounce of sadness in my heart for them. You did what you had to do."

"Fuck." His eyes slam shut and I watch his body shudder before he lets out a deep sigh. "You fucking knew, you knew and still say you love me?"

"Mason, I told you before. I see you. I love you, all of you, the good the bad and everything in between." I chuckle, "You're so ridiculous."

He laughs then too, the tension in the room absolutely evaporates, "Me, what kind of weirdo falls in love with a fucking murderer."

"Last I heard they call her Ice."

A deep scraping sound captures my attention, someone is coming in the door.

"Isley, please you need to fucking listen to what I told you, when they let you out, just run ok?"

"What the hell, didn't I just tell you …"

"Woman, I love you too. I can't focus on getting me out if you're here. Run, I'll get myself out. Do you hear me! Get to my club. If the guys aren't already out looking for me tell them. Do you understand?"

I stop for a second to absorb what he said, finally he admits that he has feelings for me. I want to reach over and smack him upside his head for taking so long.

"Yeah, I hear you."

The door opens and the man with tattoos on the side of his head comes in.

"Guys guess what, my friend has finally shown up. We have some questions that we need to ask you."

"Bull, you can ask me whatever you want. I'll tell you everything, but-" the man cuts Mason off.

"Nah man, not you. We have questions for her." He smiles and grabs the back of my chair.

"Wait what the fuck are you talking about, she doesn't know anything!" Mason pulls at his restraints hard and he yells at the man who is dragging me away. "She doesn't know shit." I see Mason panic and it just heightens my own fear. Oh, this is going to be bad. "Let her fucking go! Don't you put your damn hands on her!"

As the door opens and Bull pulls me out, Mason's eyes fall to mine. "I'm here Ice, I got you."

I believe him, if there is one thing I know no matter what happens Mason will take care of me.

"Oh, aren't you a pretty one?" The man drags me into another room and there are a few men there.

"Stay the hell away from me." I lean as far back in the chair as I can.

"Baby, don't be so mean. We just want to talk to you."

"For what, Mas … I mean Yang was telling you the truth, I don't know anything."

"I don't think that's the truth. I think you know more than you realize." Bull pulls my chair and straddles my lap. His warm breath licking at my face.

"What do I know? What do you want from me?" I move my head to the side, trying to get as far away from him as possible.

"I want you to call Jameson."

"Jameson? From the Club." I think back on the few people there that I have actually met. Wasn't Jameson the VP?

"The VP? Yang will get him for you. I don't have any way to get in contact with him."

"See that I don't believe, the other girl said the same thing. I've seen you coming in and out of that clubhouse. You know how to get in contact with him."

"I don't. I only go there for Yang. Get it from him."

"Unfortunately, that's not going to work out. Are you sure you don't want to help me?"

Tears fall down my face, but I turn so that I'm looking right at him. "I don't want to do anything for you. Now get the hell off me." I snarl at him before I hack up a huge glob of phlegm and spit it directly in his face.

He laughs and gets off my lap. "Oh, another fighter. That other girl is the same. She's still fighting. I don't think she'll last much longer though. I wonder how long it will take for you."

I look around, the men are all moving closer to me. Within a second, they are clawing and pulling on me. They tear my clothes off and throw me on a hard metal surface.

"No! Fuck you! Get off! No!" I scream and kick with all I have, but there are too many of them. There is no way that I'm going to be able to get away. Four of them hold me down and another holds a cloth over my face. Everything goes pitch black for a second before frigid water starts pouring on me. I try to scream out, but the second that I do water floods my mouth. I kick and swing my head from side to side trying to find at least one place where I'm able to catch a breath. There are a few places that are not as bad as the rest, but there is always some type of water trying to force its way down into my lungs. Finally, when they move the cloth, I cough up all the water before I scream again, trying to get them to get off me.

My eyes catch a glimpse of Bull right as they bring the cloth back up to my face. He's talking to a man in a wheelchair, he shoots me a smile before the both of them leave the room to the bastards torturing me. Letting them have their way with me.

CHAPTER 21

YANG

"Bull!" I yell for him again and continue to try and get myself out of my binds. I can hear her screaming. I don't know what they are doing to her, but it sounds like she is in agony. Every time she stops it feels like my heart stops at the same time. I've never been so relieved to hear a person scream in pain before in my life. If she's screaming that means she's still alive. "Bull! I'll tell you everything you want. I'll give you everything! Just fucking stop!" I yell for him, but no one has been back since he took Ice out of the room. Why the fuck is he doing this shit?

The screaming stops again and I stop moving, trying to strain and see if I can hear anything. After a minute goes by and I still don't hear her making a sound, the panic inside builds. "Come on, babe. Say something. Please let me fucking hear you. Please, please, please." I beg softly just wanting to hear her again.

Another minute passes and nothing. Fuck I can't lose her. Not now. Maybe this is what I deserve, but I don't think I'll be able to bear it. "Bull! Come fucking back!"

When I hear nothing for another minute, I am absolutely desperate to get out of the chair. If I could reach my arm, I'd fucking chew it off to get to Ice.

My foot taps incessantly, but I make sure not to do it very hard. A loud metal scraping sounds and the door finally opens. I see Bull coming in and something behind him, but I don't pay attention, "Motherfucker, what are you doing to her? Why can't I hear her anymore? What the fuck are you doing? What do you want?" The questions come out in rapid succession.

"Easy now, you're going to wear yourself out. Don't worry she's not dead. The boys haven't finished having their fun with her yet."

My fucking heart drops at the sound of that. They were abusing her. They had my woman in the next room over and they were hurting her. I'm stuck here with no way of helping her. So much for being there for her.

"What do you want? Why do all this and not tell me what you want?"

"This? Oh really, we don't want anything from you. We just want you to suffer knowing that you failed someone you loved. I wonder how long she'll last?"

There is something metallic behind him, but I still don't know who or what it is? I see wheels, but that's it. I lean over trying to look behind Bull.

"That's right, I never let you see my friend. I have to thank you. If you guys hadn't blown me off so many times, I probably would have never found him." He steps to the side and a fucking ghost appears in my face.

169

Sitting there in a wheelchair with no legs, a horribly scarred face, and death in his eyes is René. He is alive and well. From the look of what's going on here, he is out for blood.

"Motherfucker. What do you want? I can get you anything you want René. You know I can." On cue the screaming starts again from the other room. With the door open it's much louder. My body recoils from the sound. Ice sobs and screams. I hear metal banging and then it sounds like she is gurgling. Oh God is that blood? Is she suffocating?

"René what do you want, just fucking tell me!"

He rolls into the room, "I want you to listen helplessly as we rip your woman to shreds. Unfortunately, I think we may have to cut that short. For some reason, the members of your club have all just run out of the clubhouse like there's some sort of rush. I don't want to wait around for that party. Your woman though? Yeah, I'll keep her alive for a while. String her out then offer her to my guests for a good time. She's pretty, they'll get a kick out of messing that sweet face up." He turns his wheelchair and rolls out of the room with Bull on his tail. Now we know who the cash roll is.

A second later another door opens and I hear Ice screaming and cursing. "No, please let me go." I see a man walking backwards. When he turns to walk down the corridor, he has Ice by the foot and is dragging her naked body on the dirty ground.

"What the fuck! Get the hell off her!" I pull again, feel the thick steel handcuff cutting into my arms and waist. "Isley! Ice! Fuck babe, Ice!" I scream for her as she rolls on the ground and reaches for me. She claws at the ground, trying to find anything to stop her captor.

"I swear to fucking God I will kill all of you, let her fucking go!" My heart is about to explode through my chest I'm screaming so loud.

"Mason, help, please … oh please. Mason!" Her cries are desperate and hysterical. She kicks and manages to land a nice blow on the man dragging her. Another man that is behind her pulls his foot all the way back and kicks her as if he were kicking a field goal. The force is so strong that her small body picks up off the floor slightly and slams into the wall. The screaming has stopped and now she is gasping loudly like she can't breathe.

"Ice, stay with me, fuck. Please babe." I drop my head when they pull her to the end of the hallway and turn the corner. Another door opens and closes, I hear nothing else. She's gone. I just got her and she's gone.

Time seems to stop as my mind does its best to shield me from the absolute devastation that I feel right now. I'm almost delirious as my mind plays back memories of me with my family. Memories of Christina and I horsing around. Memories of my time in the military and with my club. Anything to get away from thinking about the fact that they stole my woman from me.

I almost didn't recognize it when I felt the earth shaking beneath my feet, not realizing that the calvary had shown up.

Ever since Mark was kidnapped and killed, Archer had all of us equipped with tracking devices. One sewn into the lining of my kutte, one on my bike, and the another on the inside of my boot. Someone must have told them that I was missing. I hadn't been expecting anyone to show up for a long while. I knew they would come; they had just come too late.

The shaking gets stronger and then I hear a group of bikes come to a stop. I don't see any windows in the room I'm in since they put bags on our heads when they brought us in. All I know is we were in some kind of lumber yard.

"He's fucking here!"

"You dumb fuck Shyne, there is nothing here!"

I hear them arguing, they must not be able to find me. The tracker only brings you to within a few dozen feet or so.

"Bro, I know how to fucking read a map and I can see. The signal is here."

"Hey!" I scream out. "Hey!" I yell over and over, but either they are too busy arguing with each other to notice or they can't hear me. I can hear them so I would only think that they should be able to at least hear me a little bit.

I call for Bones. That motherfucker has the ears of a damn bat. If there is anyone that would register someone screaming for him it would be him.

"Bones! I'm here! Bones!"

"Come on. He's got to be somewhere else."

Fuck they're leaving.

"Bones!" I yell with all my might.

"Bro, come on."

"Wait a minute."

"We don't have time-"

"I said fucking wait a minute! I thought I heard someone call me."

I smile for the first time in hours, it's Bones.

"I don't hear anything."

I yell for him again, screaming so hard I'm sure I burst the blood vessels in my eyes.

"That's fucking him! That's him!" I hear Bones saying excitedly, "Archer! He's fucking here!"

There's footfall, I must be underneath them. That's why they think nothing is here.

"Bones, there is nothing here." It sounds like Jameson.

"Bones! I'm here! I'm underneath you. Don't you fucking leave!"

"He's underneath." Bones says.

It still seems like he is the only one who can hear me.

"We're not going to leave!" He screams back.

"Hurry the fuck up!" I yell.

"Yang, we don't see anything, but fucking logs. Are you buried?"

"No, I'm in a room. There's no windows. I'm chained to a chair."

"He's under there, he says there are no windows. He's chained to a chair." I hear more footfalls, but it sounds like they are going too far away.

"That's too far. I can't hear them running anymore." I scream back. I'm getting so fucking frustrated. The longer that it takes for them to get me the longer Ice is with the Drift

Demons and René. They will be able to disappear and I'd never know where she went. I need to get out of here now.

"He says y'all are too far!"

"Boys!" Sounds like Bones screams out. Then a hollow thudding echoes through the empty halls.

"That! Whatever that is! I can hear it!" I yell.

A loud metal scraping sounds, I hear people grunting and a loud bang as the door opens. My brothers come running down the stairs. They came for me, but I have no time to celebrate. I have people to kill.

CHAPTER 22

YANG

"Get me the fuck out of here right now."

"Shit, stop pulling you're going to cut into a fucking artery at any second." Shyne says as the whole crew of them file into the room with me.

"No, get me out! Now!" I roar at him, I turn to Archer, "They have Isley, they took her Archer. I need to go. I have to get her." That oh shit moment dawns on everyone and they start moving in double time. Clay runs out of whatever place we are in and then comes back with a crowbar. After a few hard tugs, the chains pop off and I dart out of the room.

"Yang, hold up." Jameson yells from behind me.

"No." I spit out as I run up the stairs that lead to the lumber yard. Apparently, they had dug this large under-ground hideaway and on top is a door made to look like a group of logs.

I make it to the surface and see the four by four with a tarp covering half of it. My bike must still be in there.

I race over to it and my brothers are behind me. Archer

grabs me before I can get a hand on my bike. I tear my arm out of his grasp.

"Don't ask me to wait. Don't tell me to stop, because I won't. She's my woman, Prez. My kutte means everything to me, but I'll lay it at your feet right now if you try and stop me."

He shakes his head, "No one is stopping you, but we don't even know who we're looking for."

"We do," I look over to Jameson, "It's René."

"Bullshit!"

"I saw him with my own eyes. He's alive and pissed the fuck off."

"Shit, let's move." That is all we need to hear and the group of us grab our bikes and roll out. There is only one way to go. If we cut through the backroads, we could catch them.

We push our bikes to the absolute limit and manage to catch up to a bunch of cars. The two cars that had followed us from the alley are at the end of the line.

"Them! That's them!" I wish I could fly. She's so fucking close.

"We have to stop them before the next turn off or they'll be on the open road and they can split." Jameson yells out.

"Take the tires out!" Shyne replies.

I shake my head no; Isley was still in there. If the car flipped, she could get hurt. Archer looks at me he must know what I'm thinking. He slows down right beside me.

"Either we stop them or she's gone. It's the only way."

Fuck! I knew he was right. "Alright." I give my consent. I didn't have any weapons with me.

So, I had to rely on my brothers to take care of this for me.

Shyne pulls his gun and starts shooting. The car in the back fishtails before it skids headfirst into a tree. A large branch spears through the car going through the driver's midsection. I slow for a second, but it's not René or Bull. Jameson stops where I am while everyone else follows the rest of the cars. He hands me his gun and I shoot the other man in the head. Ice wasn't in the car with them so he didn't matter. Bullets are now flying between the cars and us. The cars move fast, but they don't have the agility that we do. I jump on my bike, speed back up and join the rest of the guys as they try to stop the rest of the cars. We weave in and out, and start shooting at a dark green challenger. I look through the back window and see the driver turn around. It's Bull.

"That's Bull! The green car!" I push my bike harder, but just as I do the challenger zooms forward getting in front of two cars just barely missing them. The car Bull had cut off swerves and knocks into the other. The two cars jam together and spin out. The both of them meld together and skid on the small road. They smash into trees and one of the cars erupts in flames. I keep the green car in my sights, but as I am about to ride past the two cars, I hear my name being screamed.

"Mason!" I break and look at the car. Ice is banging on the window trying to break it as smoke rolls over the body of the cars.

"No, fuck no! Shit!" I abandon the chase on Bull and get to Ice as fast as I can. Only I can already see the flames inside the car and she stops banging at the window.

"Oh God, not again." Clay is running beside me a slightly

glazed look over his eyes. We had witnessed someone being burned alive before. It's not anything any of us would ever want to see again. Everyone else has followed my lead. Fuck Bull, we need to get Ice out.

Shyne runs to the front of the car, but the door is dented in.

"You have to pull her out now!" Jameson yells out as he puts his hand up to shield his face. The flames were getting intense. I try the back door, but it's locked.

I take the gun, point it at the back window and angle it so the shot will go towards the back of the car and not anywhere near where she could be. The glass explodes and I reach in to open the door, the fire shoots out. Somehow, I see her on the floor of the car not moving and covered in soot.

I grab her and pull her naked body out. I run with her in my arms away from the flames and lay her on the ground. She's not breathing.

"No, Isley." I put a hand to her neck and feel nothing. What the fuck am I supposed to do? I want her eyes open, but I can't think.

"Move!" Clay pushes me back and starts pumping on her chest. "Get on her mouth and blow into her mouth every time I say." He orders and I shake the panic out of my mind. Good. I know this step, CPR. I can do that.

I get her in the right position and wait for him to say.

After three rounds of compressions and breathing, the most glorious sight I have ever seen appears in front of me. Isley's eyes blink open and they lock onto mine. She coughs and dark black mucus comes up. I turn her over, but she keeps on coughing and struggling to breathe.

"Hospital." Jameson calls out.

"What about Bull and René?" Lex asks.

"They'll be back. We'll be ready for them." Archer hops on his bike. I pull my shirt and kutte onto Ice. I load her onto my bike the same way as before. Except I had to use one hand to hold her tight to my body. She was still breathing, but she was slipping in and out of consciousness.

I kiss her head and whisper to her the entire way to the hospital, letting her know that I was here and that I would never fucking let her go again.

CHAPTER 23

YANG

The ride to the hospital is dangerous with her on my lap like that, but even the doctor that was there said it was so much better that we didn't wait for someone to get to us. They took her back right away and start working on her. She's suffering from smoke inhalation and would need to have a skin graft for her side and a part of her back. I stay in the hospital with her for the entire surgery. I wasn't going to leave her no matter what. The guys went back to the clubhouse to get the next steps of whatever we would have to do in order. Now that we knew for sure that it is René who is behind this, I'm sure Archer will call for a lockdown. I'm not going to be locked down, not without Ice.

The elevator opens and I hear someone running. "Isley! Where is she! Ice!"

"Ma'am! You can't be screaming in here!"

I stick my head out of the waiting area, "Christina." I call out to her.

"Oh God. Mason, oh God." She breaks down and runs straight into my arms.

"When they came back and you guys weren't with them, I didn't know what to think. Are you ok? Where's Ice? What happened?" She grabs my face looking me over quickly before curling back into my arms. I look over her shoulder. The nurse that was just about to scream on her nods and goes back to what she was doing. She must see things like this all the time. At least she wasn't going to have to deal with my sister.

"Come on." I pull her into the waiting area and sit down with her on the couch. "We will be ok. She was in a bad fire, gonna need a few grafts, but she'll live."

"Ok, ok, that's good. What's happening now?"

"Surgery. It'll be a couple of hours though." I sit back in the couch, trying to relax and remind myself that Ice is strong and will make it through this.

"You going to stay? They seemed pretty freaked out over there at the club."

"I'm not leaving her. Never." I reply.

"Hmm, so you gonna admit you love her yet or does some other equally traumatizing thing have to happen?" Christina sits back with me.

"I love her Chris, truly I do. This shit's going to be weird for you, isn't it?"

She shrugs, "Not really, I mean, Ill vomit the first few times I see you two kiss. Oh, and she's not allowed to tell me about your boy parts-"

"Man parts, I'm a grown man kid."

Christina gags exaggeratedly and I laugh.

181

"Yeah, she's not allowed to tell me about any of that, but I always knew it was a possibility."

I nod my head, "Did you tell her about the Wellsley boys?"

She freezes and turns in my direction, "No, I would fucking never. Oh my God, did you tell her?"

"No, she overheard. She said she used to sneak in the house and was in my room when I came to tell you. She knew everything."

Christina puts her hand to her mouth and a big tear falls from her eye, "She knew this entire time?"

"Yeah."

"Fuck, I knew she was the best. I may try and take her for myself. Girls like that don't come around very often." She leans back and wipes her eyes.

"Sorry, gotta go get your own. That one's mine."

"You need to get to the club." Christina says after a minute.

"I already told you I'm not leaving her."

"Mason, I'm here and she's not going anywhere. You need to go figure out how to keep us safe. Sitting here isn't the next step in the plan and you know it. If they came for you once they will come for you guys again. You need to be ready."

She's right. I'm a sitting duck right now, but Archer can't afford to spread us out any more than we are.

I stand up and look at my sister. "You don't fucking move you hear me?"

"Not one step. I've got my snacks, my phone, and my charger. I can live on this couch for at least a week. The second she's out I'll call you."

"Thank you for this."

"Of course. Love you bro."

"You too."

I hurry out of the hospital and get on the way back to the clubhouse. Now that Isley was in good hands, I could worry about how I was going to make René and Bull pay for what they've done to her. It'll be slow and painful.

CHAPTER 24

YANG

When I get back to the clubhouse, Archer is on the phone and Pirate is out of his room. Capri's standing beside him in case he needs her.

"How's Ice? She, ok?" She asks me.

"Yeah, she will be." I move over to Lex. "Where's Jameson?"

"He's in with Celine. She's petrified." The man drops his head, shame covers all his features. It's technically his fault that his daughter is mixed up with someone like René. It was his bet that had gone wrong that brought him into her life.

"I know it. We're going to get him and this time we'll make sure the motherfucker is truly dead."

"You can't let your vengeance rule you Yang. We have to be smart about this shit." Bones speaks from behind me.

I turn and raise an eyebrow in his direction. "Be smart. The time for wait and see is over. If I have to be a dumbass to take out the man who terrorized my woman then I'll be that."

"I'm with you there. Time for all these fucking rules to be thrown the fuck out the window." Shyne says.

"No, we won't be throwing shit out the window." Archer hangs up the phone and comes in our direction. "Shit is rough right now, but that doesn't mean we fucking abandon who we are just because we have a goddamn challenge. Either we grow or we lose. I'm not about to lose to a motherfucker like René, so it's time we get prepared for this fucking war that he is set on us having. I got hold of the Boys of Djinn MC up in Maine, Wyatt was able to track the car through toll cameras. It crossed into Florida. This isn't the last time we are going to be hearing from him though, I'm sure of it. We won't be running from ghosts anymore. We're going to be fucking ready. Wire has his nomad crew, there's a few with him that are looking for temporary homes. It's time to open up our doors and see if any of them are a good fit. As for Clay and Lex, I think we need to call a vote right now."

Archer was on the move. He's always the one to play things easy. Slow everything down before he makes a decision. This was unlike him, but it's exactly what we need.

"They're already brothers to me." I say.

Everyone else says yea, but the vote isn't over, Jameson still needs to put in. "Shyne, go interrupt your VP."

The look of dread on his face is ridiculous, "If he hits me, I'm not talking to none of you bastards again."

He rushes over to Jameson's door and knocks once before opening it.

"Ah, what the fuck." Lex turns around as he sees Jameson with no shirt on. We don't see Celine, but I'm pretty sure she is somewhere in front of him doing something no father wants to see his kid doing.

"What the shit, Shyne!" Jameson yells at him.

"Jameson," Archer cuts straight through the bullshit, " Lex and Clay for full members … Yea or Nay?"

"Fuck yes! Welcome brothers!" He smiles wide over his shoulder and Shyne closes the door.

We all embrace the two of them, but it's still no time to celebrate. René and Bull are still out there on the loose and it's our job to hunt them down.

An hour passes, Bones and I go over our weapon inventory. Archer wants us to have enough weapons to last for a long while if need be. Right now, we get our guns from overseas, but we don't want to have to wait on anything.

Jameson has been back and forth on the phone with Wyatt trying to pinpoint exact locations in Florida that René might be going. Despite that, they haven't been able to narrow it down to one place. I on the other hand look for any fucking information on how we induct nomads. More protocols to put in place, new rules to follow.

An eerie hush falls over the club as everyone is busy getting shit ready.

Just as before, it's in the truly serene moments that disaster strikes.

The club phone blares and everyone stops what they are doing. No one moves as if we are all scared the phone would blow up or something. On the second ring, Clay reaches over the bar and answers the phone.

The second he presses the button to pick up the line he has to pull it away from his ear. Someone is screaming, but I can't make it out from where I'm sitting.

"Yeah?" Clay tries to speak, but there is too much yelling. He talks again, but this time keeps the phone to his ear. "Hold," He puts the phone out, "Yang."

Oh God.

I rush to the phone and the rest of the guys surround me ready to catch me if I fall. "Hello." My voice croaks out.

"Mason!" It's Christina. I relax when I realize that the person screaming on the other end is Ice. At least she's not dead, but now I want to know why she's screaming.

"What the hell is that, why is she screaming like that? You better still be in that fucking hospital."

"Yes, yes, yes we are. She came out of surgery and she just woke up. She is in a lot of pain. The docs are trying to give her pain medicine, but she refuses to take it. She's fucking delirious with pain, but refuses to let them give her medicine until she talks to you. Bro, you got to get her to take the damn medicine. She's going to fucking give herself a heart attack."

What the fuck, I should have stayed. I should be there right now when she needs me. "Fuck, put the phone near her so she can hear me."

"Ice, Isley! God damn, calm down. Mason wants to talk to you."

"Mason. It's Mason?"

"Yeah."

"Ma'am you're not stable, you need to take this." A man's voice says in the background.

"Listen I just want to tell him one thing, and then you can shoot me up with whatever the hell you want. Just give me a fucking minute!" I hear her yell back. Fucking fighter, always.

"Ice!" I yell into the phone trying to get her attention.

"Mason," Her voice gets louder as if the phone is pressed against her mouth.

"Babe, I'm sorry I'm not there. I'm on my way ok. I love you, just let them give you the meds."

"I love you too, but you need to listen to me."

"No Ice, we can talk later. Take the-"

She cuts me off, "You hardheaded bastard, listen to me!" She yells and I have to take the phone away from my ear for a second, "Look I'm tired and I'm hurting, but I don't know how much time she has."

What? Who the fuck is she? Is she hallucinating? "Ice what are you talking about. You're not making any sense."

"Mason, when I was in the room with that man, Bull. He kept asking me things about Jameson. That's your VP, right?"

Fuck she knew something. I pull the phone from my ear and hit speaker. I put my hand up to silence everyone.

"Yeah, Jameson is my VP." I answer her.

She moans likes she's in pain, "He wanted me to call him so he would come out. I don't know why."

"Yeah, the other man there has problems with Jameson."

"What about his woman, is she there with you."

"Yeah, Celine is here."

She lets out a pained breath, "Then it's someone else. They have someone Mason. Bull said that the other girl is a fighter too. That she's still fighting. That she refused to call Jameson as well. They have someone and they are hurting her, you have to find her."

CHAPTER 25

YANG

I get all the information I can from Ice and convince her to take the medicine promising that I will be there the next time she wakes up. Before I can even hang up the phone, everyone has their phones out and is doing check ins.

One by one the phones go away as they get the 'Okays' from everyone that means anything to them. Until Shyne is the only one still pacing away.

"Shyne?" Archer calls out to him.

"What time was that? When?" Shyne completely ignores Archer and keeps talking on the phone. "Why the fuck didn't you say anything!" he screams. He's crumbling right in front of us. "Shyne! Report!" Archer orders.

He pulls the phone away from his face. He turns, red rimming his eyes from tears he has yet to shed, his voice cracks, "I can't find Tink man. She's been gone for fucking days."

"What?"

"No, what! How? Are you sure?" Pirate asks.

"Where is Eps?"

"The bastard ran into some fucking cash and has been drunk. He said he didn't even realize until this morning. He hasn't seen her since the damn party we had here."

That seemed like a fucking lifetime ago. Shyne brings his phone from his ear and hurls it against the wall, shattering the small electronic device.

Shyne and Tink are cousins, but they have a relationship as close as Christina and me, in some regards even closer. I can only fucking imagine what he is going through right now.

"Let's go to her place, maybe she's there. We can at least check it out." Bones is the one to give that suggestion.

"Yeah, let's do that. Come on." Archer leads the way out and we all fucking follow.

When one of us is hurting we all hurt, and right now it's Shyne.

Shyne runs up the stairs to Tink's third floor apartment with the rest of us on his tail. She had to be there.

"Tiffany! Fuck Tiffany open up!" Shyne beats on the door not even giving her a second to open the door.

He digs in his pocket with the other hand and pulls out a set of keys. He unlocks the door and pushes it open.

We have to catch him the second the door opens. It's true, Tink is gone.

The house is ransacked and on the wall are picture after

picture of Tink tied up crying and beaten. In the center of them all, written in what looks like blood, are the words.

You lose.

"Fuck!" Shyne screams and runs to the wall grabbing at the photos.

We look around the house, but we all know there is no use. She's not here. René has her and we don't have even the first fucking clue where she could be.

"How did we not see this shit?" Jameson speaks out.

"We didn't see it, because you didn't fucking want to see it! We told you it was René running around, but you had your fucking head up your ass! We could have called lockdown earlier. We could have brought in the people we needed to fucking bring in. But you were so fucking against the idea that you'd fucking failed at protecting your woman."

Jameson squares up and goes straight for Shyne. "Who the fuck do you-" Before Jameson could even finish his sentence Shyne is swinging on him. Shyne wasn't a big dude in any form of the word, the shortest out of all of us and usually the one goofing off. He was going for Jameson as if he were going to kill him. Jameson would literally only need to push him off, but even in his anger I'm sure Jameson can see what we all see. Shyne is fucking lost. Tink is a massive part of his world, to lose her like this is devastating.

Archer quickly gets in between the two of them and subdues Shyne. "Stop, that shit isn't Jameson. That's on me. It's my fault. I could have called lockdown and I didn't. This is on me Shyne." He lets him go and Shyne doesn't say a word to Archer.

At the end of the day, no matter what call any of us make Archer is the be all end all.

Pirate calls the local authorities. Even though we're going to do our own thing finding Tink, the police also need to be aware. The officer on scene tells us that he will gather all the evidence so they can pinpoint any suspects. They don't need to. We already know who it is. René is back in the hunt to destroy us and he's already proven that we're nowhere near ready for what he has in store.

EPILOGUE
ICE

My eyes open, but I'm face down on the bed. I try to get up, but a hand pushes me back down.

"Where the hell do you think you're going?"

"Mason!" I gasp and try to get up again. The pain in my back is so fucking intense that I have to freeze. Tears pop out of my eyes and he is up reaching for the phone.

"No, wait, I'm ok. I was just surprised. I'm ok."

"Isley don't be a fucking hero if you're hurting, we have medicine for that shit."

"I'm ok for now Mason, I promise. I just moved too fast." I lay back down and just look at him, "You're here."

"Where else would I be?" He smirks at me as he pulls up a chair and sits by my head.

"What's going on with my back?" This was the first time that I was up and fully lucid. At least I hope I'm lucid. If this is all a dream I'm going to be pissed.

"You had a burn on your side and some of your back. You needed a skin graft. Doctor says it's taking very well, but you will be here for a few weeks while it heals up."

"Yikes! There go all my bikinis."

"That's right."

My heart drops at the thought of him finding me less attractive, "I can get something to cover up the scars."

He leans close to me, "I'm not talking about your scars. Those bikinis are going, because now that your mine, I'm the only one who's going to be looking at your goods."

I can't stop the smile from spreading on my face. "What makes you think I'm yours?" I roll my eyes, "I could just be looking for a one time thing. We can totally forget it the next day." I laugh at my own joke.

He grunts and kisses me. Whatever was funny suddenly completely forgotten. Now all I want is to get more of what he is giving me. I move closer, but the pain in my back fights for attention. He pulls away before I can do anymore damage.

"Sorry Ice, this'll never be a one time thing. Your mine now. Remember I did warn you. Now you have to deal with the consequences."

I settle back down on the bed, my heart's slowing down and my thighs still clenching together in search of relief for the sudden pressure that has built up in my core. "Oh yeah, and what are the consequences?'

"Me, touching, fucking, and loving you."

"Sounds like a good time, I'll take it."

He smiles again before he leans in to kiss me. I knew we would be good together even before he did. Now for the next step, figuring out what our forever will look like in his world.

EPILOGUE

TINK

My mouth pulses in agony.

They'd said I talked too much so they clamped my mouth shut. A metal cage like gag that fits over my lips and connects around my head, running from my chin up to the crown of my head. Every time I try to open my mouth dull metal needles press into my lips. It's one way to get me to shut up.

"Motherfucker! What do you mean Yemen is in jail? How is that even possible? I have a whole fucking shipment of people to be put up for auction." The man in the wheelchair has been upset for a few hours now.

Apparently, someone was supposed to come pick us up, but they never came. The man that I was supposed to be given to is in jail.

I guess that's a good thing. The longer I'm here the more time it will give Shyne and the rest of the Wings of Diablo boys to find me.

I feel something warm on the side of me. When I turn my head, I see the girl that is chained up next to me has pissed all over herself and that pee is now leaking on me.

"MMMph. Mmm. MMM!" I try to pull away and get someone's attention. My body is already raw and bruised from the constant beatings. Now I to have to sit in someone else's urine, it was too much.

"For fuck's sake is she up again. Give her another hit."

No, I should have shut up. Fuck I'd rather sit in someone else's shit than have them stick that junk back in my body.

A man walks over to me with a syringe in his hand and grabs my arm. I kick up and try to pull my arm away, but my hands are clamped to the wall above me and I can't get away. He grabs hold of my bicep and right in the crook of my elbow slides the needle into my arm. Whatever he injects me with burns.

I whimper as I can feel my body slowly begin to shut down. The pain is still there even when I sleep and it seems like they always have me sleeping. I just need to stay alive long enough for Shyne to find me. He'll find me and get me out of here. I know it. He's the only chance I have.

NEXT UP IN THE WINGS OF DIABLO

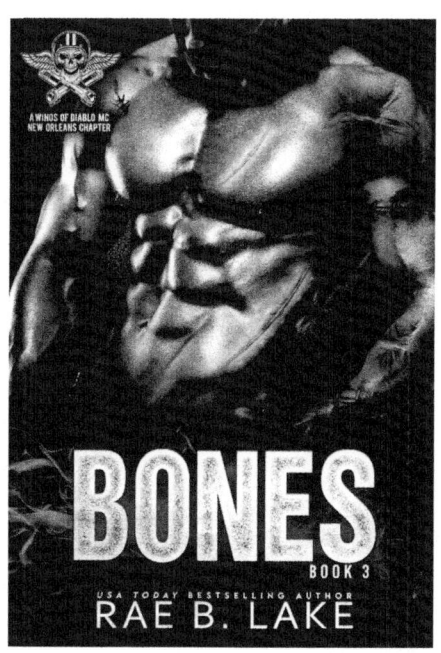

The scars are my mask and death my playground.

They say I need to heal, that I need to move on.
The pain must be part of the cure.

Pre-order Bones Today!

MORE FROM RAE B. LAKE

Wings of Diablo MC

Wire

Archer

Clean

Cherry

Prez

Ryder

Ink

Roth

Mack

Storm

Dillon

Pope

Wings Of Diablo MC - New Orleans

Jameson

Yang

Bones

Spawns of Chaos MC

Shepard

Tex

Maino

Juric Crime Family

Sven's Mark

Josip's Secret

Eve's Fury MC

Becoming Vexx

Free

Riot

Duchess

Sugar

Boys of Djinn MC

Wyatt

(Wyatt, Book 1 is in the Twisted Steel Anthology)

Cody

The Shop Series Books

His Georgia Peach

To Protect and Serve Donut Holes

On The Edge of Ecstasy

His Peach Sparkle

Royal Bastards MC
Death & Paradise

Standalones
Drunk Love

Saving Valentine

FOLLOW RAE EVERYWHERE!

FACEBOOK
READER GROUP
TWITTER
INSTAGRAM
GOODREADS
AMAZON
WEBSITE
BOOKBUB
NEWSLETTER

Printed in Great Britain
by Amazon

25893301R00121